I0626677

SURRENDERED V

By

Peggy Patrick

Copyright 2016 by Peggy Patrick. All rights reserved.

This book, or parts thereof, may not be reproduced in any form without prior written permission from the author.

ISBN-10: 0996295941
ISBN-13: 978-0-9962959-4-9

Cover Design by Charlene Raddon
http://cover-ops.blogspot.com

IN MEMORY
OF
MY ANGEL OF A STEP-MOM

ALICE LAKE

100% PURE LOVE!

SURRENDERED V

CHAPTER ONE

Carly Jones wanted to bang her frustrated head down on her desk, but knew that would only get her a sore knot on her noggin and *not* help her get out of this trip to—a *dude* ranch. "Ahhh!" She did *not* want to do this! There wasn't a country-girl bone in her body. Not one!

She was a secretary, actually *the* secretary, in the office of Webber Vance, Private Investigator, in downtown Sacramento. She wore four-inch plat formed stilettos and silk suits to work, slacks out to dinner and gauzy silk lounge wear around her contemporary up-scale apartment that was walking distance from her job. She was perfectly content with the routine she had settled in to over the past year.

At age 22, she had landed a job that paid her enough to move out on her own. Not that she particularly needed to leave home. Life with her parents and three older brothers was a good life of love and respect, laughter and fun—never ending practical jokes and pranks that almost always came in fours.

Her siblings and dad were a household riot, especially during her younger years. Her mom always claimed that she lived for the late-night hours when everybody was asleep. But, Carly's favorite memory of her mom was of her bending over in front of the kitchen sink and holding her stomach from laughing so hard at the boy's antics.

But the three *comedians* had each left for college, then the two oldest, Van and Langley married and moved to other states. Dawson was still single, working and living in Sacramento. Carly, the family baby, had finally emptied the nest when she insisted it was past time for her to spread some independent wings. And she loved every minute of living on her own and her job.

Until this! *This,* being a small stack of cash with a note pad lying on top with written instructions to head to the nearest western store and get cowboy boots, jeans and hat. *Dude up* the note said. "Ahhh," she growled.

Carly had always hated getting dirty and High Point Dude Ranch out of Jackson Hole, Wyoming sounded dirty—smelly, as in cow poop and mud and sweat. And this was happening to her all because her boss got a bad vibe?

Leonard Doss had blared into the office a few days ago demanding, "where's Vance?"—throwing his weight around as though he owned the place and the people in it. He wanted his run-away son found—his twenty-four-year-old son who needed to come home and be a man for a change. Get law school behind him so he could take his place in the Doss family law firm. The man was a cigar chewing tyrant for the hour he'd spent pacing through Mr. Vance's office. He'd cursed and shouted, "I don't have time to spare searching for the lazy ass, but my money can find him." Then he'd slammed a wad of one hundred dollar bills onto the P.I.'s desk along with a business card. "This will get you started. Find him. Call me." Then he stalked out.

Three days later, Mr. Vance told her he may have stumbled on to Mr. Doss's son. The name, Doss, popped up on a social media page belonging to a Reeny Brandon who was listed as a co-owner of a dude ranch in Wyoming. There was no other information, just this last name. Slim to no chance, Carly thought. And *she* had to go incognito and snoop out the information that her boss wanted to know. If the person at the Wyoming ranch indeed was Doss's son, why did he disappear from his family? Which hit her as very odd since the son of Leonard Doss was an adult. By law, he could disappear if he wanted to.

Carly had never seen her boss concern himself with those things. He normally gathered his facts, reported to his clients and exchanged his find for a pay day. Her job was to keep the client files updated. She knew how he worked his business— not to mention, he always did his own investigating. Never had she been sent to do his snooping.

Mr. Vance's office door opened slowly. He peeped out at Carly before coming out to face her. After her initial reaction to his chunking down the cash for a cowgirl outfit and his rather gruff instructions for the assignment he'd given her, he had headed briskly into his office and shut the door. He must have figured she needed a few minutes to absorb the new assignment. Especially after she yelled "No way, Hosea," at his retreating back.

He was always straight forward, no nonsense—so seeing him peep out of the partly opened door before approaching her desk caught her off guard.

"You'll be there and back in no time, Carly. Buy some boots and pack a bag. Your plane leaves tomorrow afternoon."

Her mouth gaped at the same time her large green eyes spread even wider. "But—you always do this part. I mean—*you're* the investigator. I don't know anything about—about P.I.ing."

"I can't go, Carly. I need this information before—as soon as you can find it out." The lines in his face deepened in a desperation that stopped her next argument and popped a new thought.

"Mr. Vance, do you know these people? Are they…"

"I know of them," he answered quickly. "I have to be gone the rest of the day and for maybe a week, maybe less. Can I count on you, young lady?"

She could only stare at him. His plea was edged with pain, but she didn't know if it was physical or emotional. He seemed to be struggling to cover up that part.

Webber Vance had held up exceptionally well for his seventy years. She had guessed his age at middle fifties a year ago when he had hired her. His clothes fit his well-defined muscled physic in a way that never failed to draw the ladies' eyes. And young eyes, at that. Not hers though, and thankfully he wasn't the flirty type. His salt and pepper hair was thick and now that she was staring hard at him, she noticed that something about him had changed recently. How had she not noticed that the man she practically lives with eight to ten hours every week day was suddenly looking too thin and more like his age.

She picked up the stack of cash and dropped it into her purse in the bottom drawer of her desk. "I'll shut everything down here before I go home tonight, since neither of us will be back for a few days."

"No. You go now. I'll close up." He reached across the desk and squeezed her shoulder. She looked up at him and felt her heart grab when his eyes pooled. "Thank you, Carly. This means a lot to me." He turned, walked to his office and closed the door behind him.

One Day Later

The grin on Beau Doss's face matched the popping high-five he exchanged with Andy Parker as the pair rode their horses to a stop beside each other. It had taken Andy a full day to coax Beau onto the back of a horse. That was over six months ago and here he was…riding, *and roping,* like he was born for it and feeling real proud of himself, too.

"Woo-yeah…rope that cow right now, Mr. Beau!"

"Accidents happen," he grinned and darted his eyes at Andy.

"My hind end! A cowboy can't throw a loop like that and catch a cow from the back of a speeding train by accident."

Beau reddened beneath his borrowed Stetson straw and watched the ground in front of their horses. "Thanks."

"Think I'll pronounce you graduated from dude to cowboy and call it good before you get better than me."

He laughed. "Naw. You're safe enough."

At almost eighteen years old, Andy had earned a top hand position on the neighboring Double OO Ranch as well as in the local rodeo. He'd earned the respect of the best of the best after beating a few of the pro ropers who came in for the local rodeo. Secretly he had dreamed of the glittery lights and crowd applause of the rodeo world. He'd never talked about it much, but the draw inside him was stronger than ever these days. He'd been swinging a calf rope around since he was five years old…Felt like a third arm now.

"Good job today, men." Les Kane, foreman for the Double OO Ranch, rode up and stopped in front of his day work cowboys and shook their hands. "Can I count on either of you tomorrow? In fact, I need you the rest of the week."

"I'll be doing dudes all week," Andy answered. "Dad said we have kids coming so I'll be wearing my lifeguard hat at the swimming hole and my *OMG hat* for some first-time horse riders."

They all laughed out loud

"Yeah…seems like a few days ago you wore that hat for me…on Poncho, no less." Beau grinned, his face pink, remembering his first horse ride on the ranch *baby-sitter* pony.

"It *was* a few days ago and here you are…roping alongside the one what taught ya!" Les nodded toward Andy, then slapped Beau on the shoulder. "Makin a good hand, too. Comin tomorrow?"

"I'll be here."

"Good. You two turn your horses out and have a good evening." Les bumped his horse with a spur and loped back to help his hands finish up for the day.

The pair rode back to the Double OO barn...groomed, fed and turned out their mounts in an outdoor pen, then shared a five-mile ride back to High Point Dude Ranch in Andy's old ranch truck. Surprisingly, the old six was still holding its own. It was probably the oldest living thing on the ranch, but as long as it took Andy wherever he wanted to go...he was happy.

He would graduate high school in another month. Summer school the past two years gave him a light senior year with only three classes in this final semester. The rest of his time was spent helping to run his parents dude ranch or doing day work for the neighboring Double OO.

With his eighteenth birthday and graduation about to happen, Andy was feeling the call more and more to spread his wings and check out life outside of Jackson Hole, Wyoming. College was a big topic with his mom and stepdad, Laura and Jesse Brandon. They were urging him to apply for college...somewhere...but, truth was, he was tired of school. And he was more serious about rodeoing than he had the nerve to tell them about just yet.

He pulled up and parked in front of the barn. "You coming in for supper? You know Mom always plans for you."

"Aww…naw, I think I'll turn in. I have plenty to eat in the cabin. Thanks though." Beau shot him his famous grin, got out and stiff- legged to one of the dude ranch cabins he was renting from the Brandons.

His was one of five new ones that had only been built in the past year and a half. That made ten altogether and several full-sized teepees for dude ranch guests during spring, summer and fall. Since he had come here during the winter shut-down, he could choose any cabin for himself. He took one that was farthest away. For one, he didn't want to be a bother to this family and two, he was shy and used to keeping to himself. The only reason he stayed here at all was because his job as a cowhand allowed him to pay his own way.

It was nearly dark when he closed his door and flipped on a lamp beside the little reclining loveseat. A steaming shower and Dagwood sandwich later, he flopped down in it and reclined.

This was Heaven…if there *was* such a place. He looked around the room like he'd done a million times. It had certainly had a woman's touch with the frilly white curtains on the windows. A red and white checkered table runner on the breakfast bar with an old quart milk bottle filled with yellow and white silk daisies set in the center of it. The kitchen was stocked with pots and pans, dishes, and toaster and microwave. And of course, a full cook stove and refrigerator. Fresh towels were always set just inside his front door where he left his used ones. He washed his own personal clothes in the Brandon's utility just inside their kitchen. He just added a little extra to his rent each month to pay for the water he used. Mrs. Brandon told him that wasn't necessary, but he paid it just the same.

His bed was full size with a patch-work quilt on top of cool light blue sheets. Mrs. Martha Walton insisted on the sheets being piled with the dirty towels every Saturday morning.

Now *that* lady didn't make any bones about what she did or didn't want out of him. She told him how she wanted things done, and if he didn't do it that way, *your butt's mine*, she'd told him.

He laughed aloud at the remembrance. The lady was hilarious, but he knew she was dead serious at the same time. He found himself going out of his way to hang around her when he saw her working around the cabins. She was such a direct contrast to anyone in his own family. In fact, so was everyone else around here.

It was a rare thing these days for him to think about his family. But when he did, there wasn't much emotion that came with it. His parents were both lawyers, as well as his only sibling, a twin sister.

Juliette had followed the family tradition of law school, and then partnered with their dad in the Doss Law Firm. Beau had no interest in that field and after high school graduation, he was escorted to the door of the posh family mansion as a manipulative move to force him to sign on for law school. It was their way or the highway…literally. But he couldn't concede in his own heart to try living their life. He had not a clue one what he wanted out of life, but he did know what he didn't want. The endless dinner parties, drinking and hobknobbing with the biggest diamond rings and mink coats in town had captured every moment of his parents' lives...When they were home, that is. Otherwise, he never had any idea where they were or when they would come back home. His sister enjoyed the finer side of it all. But after two days of sleeping on the front porch, his only way back inside was to agree to enroll in college. He did that, and completed two years of basics, still without a clue where he was headed, but knowing it wasn't law school. In a last-ditch effort to get him to comply with their wishes, they took his car away and once again, rendered him homeless and afoot.

That was the day he walked away, worked for a local garden supply company until he earned enough for a few personal needs that fit easily into a small backpack and a bus ticket out of Sacramento.

But to where? He had taken a seat in the bus terminal feeling like a lost and unloved stray mutt. On the seat beside him lay a small cardboard poster with snowcapped mountains in the background and pictures of cowboys riding bucking horses. He had picked it up and studied it a full minute before deciding that would do. He bought a ticket to Jackson Hole, Wyoming.

He had stepped off the big greyhound after dark and one block from a neon sign that said *The Burger Gettin' Place.* He was starved, and minutes later after a plate load of fries, cheeseburger and a tall iced tea, he counted his remaining money. He might have just enough for one night in a motel. That's when he met Andy Parker. He never did understand how he had ended up at High Point Dude Ranch with a furnished, fully stocked cabin to live in and a job starting the next morning before sun-up...all in the space of an hour after the bus left him standing in the street of Jackson Hole. *So you're the one,* Andy had said when he appeared suddenly at his table. Then he introduced himself and proceeded to tell Beau about his family's dude ranch. He asked no questions about his life...where he had come from or his job experience.

And here he was three months later, reclined in a comfortable enough easy chair after a hot shower and supper, an aching backside from hours in a saddle and contented with life in a way that was foreign to him. Once he had conquered his paralyzing fear of horses, he seemed to take to riding, then swinging a rope as though he'd done it all his life. Who knew? And there was nothing he wanted to do more than rise earlier than the sun and cowboy all day. *So you're the one.* He made a mental note to ask Andy what he had meant by that.

He was almost afraid to ask too many questions about the good fortune that had swept him off his feet his first hour in Jackson Hole. His life on this ranch was like one of those, *too good to be true*, moments, that had now turned into months.

He and his twin, Julie, had pretty much raised themselves. She'd spent a lot of time at friends' homes while he hung out alone most days when he wasn't in school. The seclusion of this little dude ranch cabin was comforting, rather than lonely. Not that he liked being reminded of his *alone* boyhood in the Doss mansion, but he was simply used to being by himself. There was a kind of security in that.

But at times, he watched the interaction of the Brandon family, the relationship between Jesse and Laura and their three kids, Andy, Anna Leigh and Jesse, Jr. So much laughter and silly pranks—fun and games. Hard work, as well, but a lot of togetherness. He envied their closeness at times, but when they attempted to pull him into the middle of their family doings, he shied and kept his distance. No one got angry at him. No one pushed or ridiculed, or chunked him out the ranch gate. They just let him be. He wondered if Andy had a clue just what he had here. This family…this life.

Beau raised both arms high above his head and reared back in his recliner. He stretched until his whole six foot, four-inch lanky frame was stiffly horizontal. He groaned as his muscles drank in the fresh oxygenated blood. "Ahh…yes!" *How can a simple ten second stretch feel so good?*

How could *he* feel this good with his life? Suddenly it seemed, he went from utterly dependent on the provision of his absent parents, extreme loneliness, having no direction to go…to this. It was as if *this* had come to meet him when he stepped off that Greyhound bus in Jackson Hole…after blindly travelling hours from California. He hadn't given it much thought until this minute. Thinking back now, it seemed incredible. So much so, that it couldn't have been a mere coincidence. Could it? *So you're the one. You're the one.*

Beau jumped and left his pondering behind him in the recliner when a loud knock banged his door.

"Beau?"

He opened the door to find Andy a little breathless and in a hurry.

"I need a favor, man. Mom and Dad are out for the evening. I plumb forgot. I can't leave the kids and Jesse, Jr. is already asleep. I promised to help Anna Leigh with homework and I forgot to tell anybody about Ms. Jones."

"Whoa, slow down." Beau was laughing at his animated *help me, somebody* story.

"Okay, so you'll do it?"

He doubled over then. "Do what? You haven't told me anything yet."

"Pick up Ms. Jones from the airport. In Jackson. Over an hour ago!"

"Seriously, Andy?"

"Yeah, she's a dude ranch guest. I was supposed to pick her up at six. It's already seven. Take my old truck. It's gassed up. Here's the flight information." He slapped a small paper off a note pad into his hand. "Thanks, man. I owe you," he yelled as he turned and headed for the main house to care for his young siblings.

In less than three minutes, Beau headed through the ranch gate. He didn't bother to change his heavily wrinkled t-shirt and sweats, just grabbed his dirty canvas shoes. Too late, he noticed his fresh washed hair sticking out in nine directions. He rubbed at it to no avail. A quick glance around the pickup cab didn't find so much as a ball cap. Great! He was parking the truck in the airport garage when it dawned on him that he had no clue what Ms. Jones looked like or even how old she was.

All ages came to the ranch to experience the cowboy life. He guessed he could always hold up a sign with her name on it. Well, part of her name, anyway.

Carly realized she was gritting her teeth only after her jaws began to throb. If her teeth broke off and fell out, she figured she'd fit right in with this bunch of country bumpkins out here in cow patty America. She'd been waiting over two hours for Hop Along Earp…or… Maverick, to pick his way to the airport to get her. When he did show up, she planned to give him a large slice of her bored, disrespected and angry mind!

She glanced up from the novel she'd been trying to keep her thoughts on. There…case in point! The Beetle Juice look-alike leaning against the wall just a few yards from where she sat and looking like Buttermilk the bull had just bucked him off and dragged him here! If she wasn't so furious, she would have laughed at her own description of him. But almost instantly, she felt badly. Poor guy. Her conscience stabbed her heart at poking fun, even in her head, at a man who was obviously down on his luck. Wouldn't it be a kick in the rear if he was Riley Doss. She could shake his hand while secretly pressing a twenty into his palm, then hop the next jet for home. Mission accomplished.

Well, almost. She would have to wait long enough to ask why he dropped off the planet…except that Mr. Vance wanted this information without Riley Doss knowing about it. So… maybe she could…

Realizing how ridiculous her mental ramblings were, she raised her kindle reader to her face and groaned behind it. Anyway, she needed to be on the look-out for a sophisticated clean cut type when she got to this ranch. The Doss family was well-to-do, up-town folks. He wouldn't have turned into Beetle Ju... *Stop it,* she inwardly yelled at herself.

Then she remembered the picture of Riley that Mr. Vance had laid on her desk. Stupidly, it was still lying there, but she had studied it well enough she thought. He was thin, almost frail, with a short haircut. Average looking, preppy, Ivy League type. The more she thought about it, the more she knew this trip was going to be a dead end. Riley Doss would not have come to a Wyoming barnyard to start a new life. It didn't fit. He was a city boy. And on top of that, no one had shown up from the ranch to pick her up. Her feet hurt, she was starved and too angry to hook back into the novel on her kindle. The next flight to Sacramento would happen in another hour and she planned to be on it. Mission finished!

Beau decided he wasn't going to find Ms. Jones standing here waiting to spot a lost *dude* walking by. He'd been fairly sure he could spot her easily enough. Dudes that came to the ranch could be wearing just about anything imaginable... except for the boots. Every last one of them *always* arrived wearing cowboy boots. *New* cowboy boots. But he hadn't spotted a single female in the airport that fit the mold.

He cut his eyes for another quick look at Ms. High Class sitting across the aisle in the waiting area. That definitely wasn't her, but he was enjoying sneaking a glance now and again. Her platinum blonde ponytail was the only school girl looking thing about her. He recognized the expensive cut and material of her red silk skirt and silver angora sweater that she wore. Not that he was so up on women's fashions, but he'd seen this type of clothing on his sister, Juliette, and Juliette was no spendthrift. And nobody...*nobody* would be coming to vacation at a dude ranch wearing those spike heels and shiny silk stockings. Gorgeous as she was, he sighed heavily and moved on.

He couldn't think of anything else to do except have her paged with enough information that, if she was even here, she could come to him. He found his way to the nearest ticket information counter which was a good distance down the terminal. He gave the information that he knew and listened to the lady issue the page...." *Ms. Jones. Ms. Jones. Your party is here from the High Point Dude Ranch to pick you up. Please report to ...."*

"What? Seriously?" Carly sputtered. He better have a good reason for leaving me stranded for close to three hours in an airport like this. Anything could have happened to me. Carly mumbled to herself as she gathered up her overstuffed bag and purse and headed out to find this ...*cow*-boy.

***

CHAPTER TWO

Beau leaned his back against the ticket counter, arms crossed over his chest and one foot hooked over the other. He looked down the aisle one way, then the other. A number of people in obvious groups of family and friends made their noisy way past him, heading to board a flight or just getting off of one.

He had become oblivious to how he looked. He'd forgotten that his below the collar hair was sticking out and straight up. His scrunchy wrinkled clothes and dirty white tennis shoes had been basically irrelevant. It had been a long day; he was exhausted and didn't think too much about his beggarly appearance…until the frozen moment that he realized that the little classy blonde bombshell dressed to the nines in hose and heels was approaching the counter right beside him. She spoke directly to the woman working behind the counter without sparing him so much as a glance.

"Hello. I was paged to meet…"

The woman pointed toward Beau's bushy hair and stricken red face.

Carly turned fully around, then stood stunned as she stared up at him. She watched as his eyes—big, deep blue eyes, traveled down the length of her, then back up. She wanted to feel disgust at this tramp of a man ogling her, but she was too angry to feel anything other than plain mad.

"*You* are a cowboy? From the dude ranch?"

He opened his mouth, but nothing came out.

She saucily returned the body scan, deliberately letting him watch her do it.

When her eyes met back up with his, she didn't find the embarrassed and intimidated hobo, but an obvious amused smirk. Her assessment hadn't accomplished her intent of putting him in his place.

This time his voice was all there and in control. "I was expecting someone in cowboy boots, mam." He nodded down at her high heels.

"So was I," she retorted with her finest glare.

The way he was looking at her with a slight lift to his upper lip and not even trying to conceal the fact that he found her laughable and out of place, caused her back to straighten even more. If she had a mirror, she'd show him what she was looking at—Mr. wrinkled up, mucky shoe, messy-head. Oh yeah, he had a lot of room to smirk at her. Never mind those attractive blue eyes focused on her—those long dark lashes, narrow face, straight nose and a couple days' growth of black stubble. Sexy black stubble. How had she missed his handsome face earlier when he was standing near where she was seated?

He knew how he looked. She was standing there accessing his *homeless* appearance with her nose in the air. A rather cute, sculptured straight nose, a soft feminine mouth and green eyes that said she didn't want to be standing here with him right now.

Well, he'd prefer to be kicked back in his recliner and sipping hot coffee about now, too. Alone. So may as well get this show on the road and over with. He bent down and picked up her one bulging bag she'd set down beside her feet.

"Is this all you have?"

"That's it. Thanks."

He nodded approval, but wondered how somebody who dresses like she does could get by on one bag of stuff. "This way, Ms. Jones." He turned and headed out without looking back.

Carly sorely hoped this guy was just the hay forker person or whatever they called him. There had to be more intelligence on that ranch than this. One thing was for sure—this character was *not* Riley Doss. Riley was a college graduate raised in the lap of luxury, so this only served to convince her that the trip here was a futile waste of time.

And why was she not a bit surprised when he threw her bag into the back of an old farm truck that looked like it should have been retired years ago.

Beau opened the passenger door and slightly bowed, holding a hand out to assist her. When she ignored him and stepped up easily into the cab without his help, he shut the door a little louder than necessary. She ignored that, too.

He hadn't yet bothered to introduce himself and she decided she didn't care what his name was.

As soon as they were clear of the airport traffic, he decided to let her off the hook—somewhat. He wasn't angry at her, more like giving her what she deserved. The way she was looking down her nose to size him up was not his type of female.

"So, are you hungry?"

She was starved. "Yes, I am."

"It's late. Mind if we grab a burger at a drive-thru? I've got to be up for work before daylight." He kept his eyes on the road.

"That would be fine, thanks." She cut her eyes to glance at his profile. The sound of his voice—resigned, tired, made her feel ashamed of her scathing assessment of him. When did she get so high and mighty, anyway? Her parents weren't high dollar people and she was raised to treat people better than how she was treating this man.

And then again, nobody had to be three hours late to pick up a client, a lone female client, at a busy airport. That's pure irresponsible. And nobody had to dress like a bum who didn't own a hair brush. And never mind those filthy shoes. Anybody can be clean and comb his hair.

Before she finished her fresh internal angry rant, Carly had a warm paper bag dropped into her lap. A cold drink of some kind was placed into a wobbly cup holder that was attached to the dash. Then they were headed back onto the highway without one word spoken between them.

Her temper rose with a vengeance. OMG! He ordered for her and didn't even ask what she liked to eat or drink. She lifted the paper wrapped sandwich out of the bag to find it leaking and slathered with mayonnaise. She hated mayonnaise.

Beau could see her out of the corner of his eye. He watched her cram the burger back into the bag and fold her arms stiffly across her chest. Boy, was she ticked off! He didn't intentionally order wrong food for her, he just didn't ask what she liked. She apparently wasn't interested enough to talk to him and let him know, but had kept her head turned the other way. So there you go, Ms. High Class.

His sole aim was to get back to the ranch, into his comfortable bed and free of this—dude. She's all yours, Andy my friend. He had to fight to keep a grin off his face.

She shot a look across the cab of the truck that Beau was sure could have won an academy award. He figured he deserved that *off with your head* slicing blow from those glittering green blades, but darn it all—he'd lived with spoiled self-centered women his whole life. He didn't care to be caged with one of them, even for a short pick-up ride.

The past months at High Point Ranch had shown up his true goals for his life, including peace, heart-felt happy, and people around him who respected his desire to hang out on the sidelines, if he chose to. For the first time in his life, he *knew* acceptance and appreciation for whatever he was able to contribute to their lives. And they asked no more than that.

Jesse Brandon, his younger brother, Donny, Hank Walton and all their wives were as individual as red and green, yet all had something about them that was pleasantly the same. It was difficult to explain, so he didn't try. He just enjoyed it.

Beau turned his head to look at her after many silent miles. She was asleep. She faced him with her head cocked in a way that was good for a crick in the neck. Without even thinking, he put the flat of his hand against her head and cheek and gently pushed her into a straighter position.

Her eyes popped open, but he didn't immediately take his hand away. He didn't want to. Her skin was smooth against his rough calloused fingers. The fluid silkiness of her pony tail that filled his hand was unexpected—and so was the tightening sensation that grabbed his belly.

She slowly rose up straight, her hair pulling through his spread fingers. The whole thing should have been disgusting to her senses— instead it sent a shiver through her middle. What just happened?

"I...I'm sorry. I..." Confusion mingled with a jet lag drowsiness. She squared her shoulders attempting to pull herself back together, then winced and tilted her head back toward Beau.

"That's why I moved your head. Looks like I was too late."

She massaged the knot in her neck while she gave herself time to quell the fluttery wave of nerves that his touch had generated. Surely she was not *that* desperate!

No, she wasn't! This day had just been long and unforgiving in throwing one punch after another at her. Against hope, she visualized a big, plushy, warm bed in a—ugh—a remote cabin. Never mind, she scolded her own fanciful imagination.

She shot a glance at her, pain in the neck, rescuer. "Thank you. I'll be fine."

All she saw out of the windshield of the truck was black darkness. The headlights shone on a dense growth of trees along both sides of the narrow highway.

"How much farther is it?"

"Couple miles is all." He thought he heard an uneasy tone in her voice. "I'll have you tucked in for a nap in no time."

Carly's eyes grew, but she kept her focus outside the truck.

A grin split Beau's face. He couldn't help himself. She couldn't possibly know that she was about to enter the safest place on the face of God's earth. At least, that's what Andy called it—God's earth.

In minutes, they were turning into an entrance gate. The headlights bounced off the overhead sign that read, High Point Dude Ranch.

Suddenly, she was on high alert. This place was spooky—so far back in the wilderness. A knot formed and grew in her throat threatening to choke off her air. What had she let Webber Vance get her into? She didn't bother to check out this place—at least check for a website. Something!

She could feel eyes studying her, but she refused to look at the so-called *cowboy* beside her. She didn't even know his name, for pete's sake!

Yellow lights came into view to show up the front porch of an old farm house. What she could see of the house was white with a large green door. Big pots of—was it some kind of tall cactus? —decorated the small porch. Further back behind the house, Carly could see more yellow lights dotted here and there through tall trees. Cabins, maybe?

Beau pulled alongside the house and stopped. With the engine running, he threw it in park, then turned his body toward his passenger. He could see she was really scared, which took him by surprise. He suddenly wanted to comfort her—let her know she was safe.

"We're here, Ms. Jones. By the way, my name is Beau." He held out his hand to her, an attempt at a fresh start. He couldn't deal with seeing her so afraid. Alone and scared was painful. He knew.

She stared at his extended long fingers, then looked up into a warm and genuinely apologetic face. Did he have a clue how comforting this truce was right at this moment? She shook his hand and quickly pulled hers back, but not before she felt that sudden fluttering in her stomach at his touch. Again. But this time, she saw the flicker in his eyes—a slight jerk of his head at the same moment. He felt it, too.

"I'm Carly," she finally managed.

He nodded and smiled. "Well, Carly, sit tight and I'll find out where your quarters are. Be right back."

He got out and she watched him disappear around the corner toward the back of the house. By all appearances, this ranch had all gone to bed.

A moment later, he returned carrying a sheet of paper and climbed in behind the wheel. "Okay, here we go." He held the paper close to the dash lights, being as the overhead cab light was out, and studied it. "I didn't get your reservation form before I left for the airport" He glanced up and out the front windshield. "Looks like you're in number five. Odd." He seemed to be talking more to himself than to her.

He tossed the paper onto the dash in front of him and drove on farther into the ranch grounds.

She could only see parts of buildings, fences and some sort of small animal cages as they slowly continued. A covered pavilion came into view—very colorful and surrounded by lots of hanging flowers and more big pots of cactus. Past that she saw Indian teepees? For real? As her eyes quickly scanned the area, she almost felt a silly excitement at what appeared to be a real live Indian village. The teepees looked authentic and so huge. Tiny solar lights lined pathways that wound around and led up to each structure.

But that excitement quickly slammed backward and became a sharp intake of breath when Beau stopped the pickup beside a teepee that seemed to be set a short way apart from the main village circle.

The look she shot him should have slung him right out of his half-opened door. Not expecting that reaction, he paused with one leg out of the truck and did a double take at her.

"What's wrong?"

It took her a few seconds to find her voice. "Tell me you are not leaving me in this…this teepee!"

"That's what your reservation is for. Says right on it, teepee number five. Didn't you know?"

She stared at him while her thoughts hopped and skipped and tried to pull up how this could have happened. Her eyes closed in exasperation when it hit. Webber Vance. Well, this just wouldn't do.

"There was clearly a mistake made. I prefer a fully walled in cabin with door locks, please."

He rubbed his stubble jaw and squinted, mainly attempting to cover the grin creeping down his face.

"Ms. Jones," he began, and wondered for the first time if that was Miss or Mrs., "it's well after midnight and there's no way to change your accommodations tonight. You can check in at the office tomorrow. It's located at the front of the main house."

She jerked a glance sideways, then back at him. "But…I can't sleep in *that.*"

Don't you want to look at it before you decide that?"

"It's an Indian teepee, Beau!"

He burst out laughing at the high-pitched screech of his name. "Yep, believe you're right. Come on. I'll get you settled." He got out and shut the door, still laughing.

She hesitated before she finally strapped her designer bag over her shoulder and stepped out, careful not to sink her high heels into the dirt. He already had her bag in hand from the back of the truck and was waiting for her to get with the program. He was bone-weary tired and wanted to go to bed.

He walked ahead and opened the flap of leather on the entrance. She was surprised when he turned a door knob behind the flap and opened a regular solid wood door. He entered and set her bag on the floor.

Surprise didn't cover her reaction when she stepped inside. More like stunned. A bed was in there. A real bed at least two-foot-high and spread with soft white, luxurious looking coverlets of some kind. Pillows made from the same material were piled against the wall at the head of the bed. Colorful turquois and tan rugs covered the wooden floor, not dirt like she had envisioned. A small lamp lit the spacious room with a cozy yellow glow that even caused the small log dresser it set on to shine. More huge and heavy pillows graced the floor across from the bed.

Before she could ask how it was so cozy warm, a small thermostat controlled electric heater fired up. It sat inside its own three-sided cubicle, obviously fire-proof for safety. It sat beside the dresser, unnoticed until it automatically came on. That's when her eye landed on the small refrigerator that appeared to be attached to the opposite side of the dresser.

Beau watched, relieved at her obvious pleasure of her room, at least for tonight. Before she realized there was no bathroom, he figured he'd better beat her to the punch.

"Let's step back out for a second." Outside, he pointed to a well-lighted cabin just the other side of the pavilion. "That cabin is only used for a bath house for the teepee guests. There's a big sign on the door that says *occupied* on one side and *open* on the other. Just remember to flip the sign around going in and coming out. There's a lock on the door as well. Any questions?"

She should have known there would be an—outhouse. She shook her head, weary of this whole experience.

Sensing her discomfort, he backed up a step. "Look through the last bunch of trees over there." Beau raised his arm and waited for her to follow where he pointed. "See the opening there?"

She nodded.

"My cabin is just inside that space. If you need anything, that's where I'll be. It's the only cabin back there, but I'll leave the outside light on.

"Thanks."

"Well, good night, then." He got in the truck and left.

After a fast trot to the potty cabin, Carly locked herself inside her teepee and slid into a thin set of jersey sleep pants and shirt. The bed was surprisingly comfortable. She didn't know if she was more tired or more hungry. The little refrigerator was thankfully stocked with snacks and soft drinks. The hunger won out so she propped up in the plushy soft bed and feasted on peanut butter crackers and a can of Sprite.

With lights out, she snuggled down under the comforter and decided to get a game plan for herself first thing tomorrow. She needed to find out if Riley Doss was here and get back to civilization.

Beau shut the cabin door behind him before reaching around to flip on the yellow porch light. He never bothered to turn it on before, but he'd told Ms. Jones he would.

Ms Jones. Carly Jones. His first impression of her had melted away. That high falootey act at the airport was only a facade. Silk leggings, high heels and perfectly applied makeup didn't cover up the insecurities he'd witnessed on that pretty face. And she didn't appear to be here for a cowboy experience. She seemed to be out of her element on both counts. Was she on the run—trying to hide from someone?

The ranch was just opening for spring and summer guests. Very few people were here for the first weekend mainly because it was still cold weather. An unusual warm few days had just passed, but a cold front was headed down in a couple days.

He wondered how well those teepees would take a real cold spell. And why on earth did they put her in one of them and not tell her—even though it was the fanciest one. He knew there were several cabins available. Strange.

He was too tired to think about it anymore. In one more minute flat, he was piled under his quilts and out like a light.

Carly felt almost drugged with sleep, like she'd been asleep for hours. But something was pulling her back to the surface of consciousness. Finally, she woke up and sat up trying to recognize through the dark, where she was. It was eerily quiet for the first few seconds, then the howling and yelping of a whole bunch of something froze her body, except for her heart rate that was pounding nine-0.

She was in a teepee stuck off by herself! "Oh no! Oh God," she choked out behind her hands that now covered her face. Was it wolves? The squealing was endless and sounded as if they'd surrounded her.

Finally, the noise faded away, but Carly was still petrified. She was alone in a wilderness of wild animals and God only knew what else.

She got up and rushed over to turn on the lamp. Pop! The bulb blew. The darkness was trying to choke her now. She got to the door and remembered seeing two long, white terry robes hanging on a hook on the inside of the door, along with two pair of matching slippers. She grabbed a robe and slid her feet into the slippers, as she unlocked the bolt and peeped outside. Not much moonlight—it was *too* quiet now.

She fixed her eyes on the spot that Beau had pointed out to her—where his cabin set. Keeping her sight on that general area, she ran toward it. Fear had an ugly grip on her—she could barely breathe. Her heart hammered. She'd always been afraid of the dark. She'd been scared silly by three big brothers who would hide in a darkened room and jump out at her, screeching like a ghoul. It seemed to be their favorite past time, but they'd left her scarred for life. She'd never fully recovered from a fear of darkness.

There it was. She saw the porch light of Beau's cabin and raced for the door knob. It was locked.

"Beau!" She knocked with her knuckles, then pounded with her fists. "Beau!"

She spied a single window and hoped that was his bedroom. She stepped just off the small porch and pounded on the glass panes hard and loud enough to wake the dead.

"Beau!"

"What in the ...!" Beau raised up and rubbed his face before hitting the floor at a run as his brain began to register. He had no idea who or what, but he'd heard his name.

Just then the screaming yelps came again right behind her. She jumped back onto the porch and threw herself against the door at the same moment Beau jerked it open. Her momentum was such that the force surprised him and both landed in a painful heap on the floor between the loveseat and the fireplace.

Beau lay still, working hard to get his breath. He was fully aware that someone—a female someone—was spread out on top of him, her arms around his neck like a tightened hanging noose. He knew she was a she because he could hear her female voice crying hysterically.

Finally, he grabbed her arms and pulled, freeing his airways and vocal chords. She jerked her arms loose and got a second hold on him.

This time he gripped her arms and pulled hard. "Hey...stop it! Stop it!" A slight shake on her arms got her attention.

When she jerked her face up from the middle of his chest, Beau saw it was Carly Jones, stark terror almost making her unrecognizable.

"W...wolves! A pack of wolves!"

He glanced toward the open door and listened. All he could hear was her quick breaths and a whimper here and there.

"Take a deep breath, Carly. You're okay. I'm sure they're gone now."

Realizing for the first time that Beau was beneath her on the floor, she slid off to the side of him and sat up, pulling the terry robe back tight around herself. She could feel the roots of her hair burning. "I'm…so sorry." She sniffled and swiped at her wet cheeks.

"There's no harm done." *Except for a couple of dislocated shoulder blades.* He stood up, then helped her to her feet. "You okay now?"

She nodded her head, then turned to look out the door.

Beau shut the door and flipped on a lamp. "You want to tell me what happened?"

"I woke up and heard loud screaming and yelping. They sounded like they were about to tear through my teepee. I heard them more than once and I turned on the lamp, but the bulb went out and it was dark. It…it was dark."

He heard every word she was saying. She thought wolves were after her and she's scared of the dark. At the same time, he was seeing a beautiful mess of tangled blonde hair, deep sea green eyes that were wet with tears of fright and a young woman who needed someone to help her feel safe.

"Coyotes." He spoke low and calmly. "They run in packs like that and sometimes sound closer than they actually are. You're not in any danger, Carly."

Just then, he heard their yelping again and reopened the door. "Step out here." He grasped her arm when she started to back away and pulled her with him. He pressed an arm around her shoulders and stood with her on the porch while he let her hear one of the sounds he loved the most, but in the safety of his embrace. He watched her face and saw the fear leave—replaced with a big-eyed awe. He smiled down at her and she leaned closer into his side.

***

CHAPTER THREE

The wee hours of the morning air were chilly and the wind was blowing just short of a howl. Neither Carly nor Beau felt it. As they stood in the after silence that fell with the last faded yelp of the coyote pack, something magical began to warm the atmosphere around them.

Carly hadn't paid attention to how tall he was until she tilted her head back and looked up at his face. What she saw slammed a hard beat in her heart.

Beau looked down at the top of her scrambled blonde locks, unable or unwilling to look at anything else around him. His breath was shallow and uneven; his heart was racing. His reaction to this woman was ludicrous. He'd wrapped his arms around girls before, hugged them tight and shared some kisses—and more, but when Carly looked up into his face like that, everything on this earth that he'd ever thought important dissolved. Emotion stung his eyes, but he didn't blink. He turned and leaned down and kissed her lips—gently, but fully.

He felt her stiffen and slightly pull back from him. He moved his arm from her shoulders and took one step away. He wasn't going to apologize for kissing her because he wasn't sorry. In fact, a surge of protectiveness stood him up to his full height of six foot four.

"I can walk you back to your camp or you're more than welcome to finish the rest of the night here. I'll be heading out in about an hour anyway. Up to you."

"Heading out to where?"

"I do day work for the Double OO Ranch about five miles that way." He swung his arm out in front of him and noticed the blank look that replied at him. "It's a cattle ranch mostly. I help round up strays, mend broken fence—that sort of thing."

"Oh, wow. Sounds like stuff I've seen in western movies."

Beau grinned down at her, wondering at the lights that had begun to dance in her eyes. Was that for the horses and cows or for the cowboy who rode and chased them?

Right now, he desperately wanted another hour or so of sleep, but he couldn't leave her standing there. He'd prefer that she curl up with him so he could know she wasn't scared of what was left of the dark night.

"So…want me to walk you to your place?"

She'd been thinking hard about it since he'd asked the first time. She couldn't do it. The thought was even too much.

"Maybe I'll just sleep till daylight in your recliner. Then I'll have all day to get used to things."

He pursed his lips and shuffled his feet—thinking. Then shook his head. "No, ma'am, can't sleep in that thing. It's too hard on the back. But, I have an idea. Come with me." He held the front door for her, then closed it and turned the lock. He grasped her hand before turning the lights out and led her to the only bedroom in the cabin.

Suddenly she planted her feet and pulled her hand, but he held on. "Surely you don't think I'm going to sleep with you…in here…with you."

He released her hand and turned off the light, plunging the cabin into blackness. She was already standing two steps from the unslept in side of the bed which happened to be closest to the door. "Your side is right in front of you. Get in and get some sleep. I've got to do the same. Goodnight."

He rounded the end of the bed and slid under the covers. He counted silently—one, two—when he felt the covers shift slightly as she crawled in. He smiled, then passed out asleep.

She pulled the bed covers up to her neck and lay flat on her back staring into the dark room. Beau had turned his back and was about as close to his edge of the mattress as possible without falling over the side. His even steady breaths told her he was already asleep. That was a good thing. Better than good, she decided. This had to be the craziest day of her entire life. After poking fun, albeit silent, at this strange homeless looking character who was loitering in the airport, she ends up in his bed in a cabin way out in no man's land, surrounded by wild dogs and—she felt so safe. A deep sigh escaped just before she closed her eyes and slept.

When she woke up, she was alone. There was enough light in the room to tell her it was fully daylight now. The cabin was stone silent.

Hurriedly she got up and rewrapped herself in the terry robe that had gotten twisted around her. She found the front door locked which made her feel oddly—looked after. When she opened the front door, a mixture of voices, adult and children, wafted in on a chilly breeze. That's when it dawned on her that she had to walk back to her teepee dressed for bed. She had no clothes and somebody was sure to see her leaving Beau *whoever's* cabin to sneak back to her own spot. She turned around glancing through the cabin as if some clothes might magically appear. The light streaming through the partly open door landed on just that. *Clothes* draped across the back of the loveseat. *Her* clothes. The brand-new jeans she had bought for the trip and her pink Wrangler long sleeve T-shirt. Her new boots set on the floor just below the clothes. Looking a little closer, she spotted her underclothes poked between the folded over jeans. *He didn't!* He dug through her stuff! The only thing that she didn't recognize where the long white socks that were stuffed into the top of the boots.

She wanted to be furious at his audacity. To stomp and rant at the rude invasion of her privacy. This bushy-headed poop-kicker walked right into her space and handled her—her underwear!

The squeal of a child suddenly blasted through the crack in the door. Adult voices intermingled with it until she quickly shut the door and locked it. Immediately she changed her tune into one of thankfulness that she had clothes to put on to nonchalantly stroll into the mix of the people out there.

She dressed and pulled her hair back into a ponytail. There was no choice but to leave her sleepwear behind. After checking to see that no one was around, she slipped outside and strolled like she thought a ranch tourist would, relishing the countryside. And strangely enough, she was very much taken with the sights out in front of her.

She followed the opening of the concave where the cabin set to a well-beaten gravel pathway leading back in the direction she had come from a few hours before in the dark. There was a totally different feel to the sights and smells of the place in the daylight. The huge pine trees gave off a fragrance that made her breathe deeply, while the lucent sun shot rays of a clean, almost clear brilliance through the sparse openings of the high branches. Her eyes and nose enjoyed the feast until a second wave of sights and smells suddenly bombarded her senses. *Bacon! Bread!* In that instant, she recognized true hunger.

Several people were having breakfast at picnic tables under the pavilion. She headed that direction, then wondered if she needed to get her purse. Mr. Vance hadn't given her any information on what to expect here.

The corner of her eye caught the motion of a man in a cowboy hat waving his arm. He was looking her way and waving for her to come there—to an old, actual chuck wagon.

"Come and git it," he yelled.

Oh, lord yes! She almost broke into a run with a *yippee* out in front of it before she caught herself. This place seemed to want to bring out the wild in a girl—or maybe it was the hunger.

"Good morning," she said as she approached the wagon. "I'm Carly Jones." She offered her hand and the elderly old cowboy quickly slid his hand down his apron front before he grasped hers.

"Good morning, Carly Jones. Hank Walton, and welcome to the best cowboy cooking both sides of the Wind River." He tipped his used-up Stetson and grinned all the way to the blue twinkles under the brim of his hat.

"I bet it is." She chuckled and picked up an oblong Styrofoam plate off of the end of a condiment table and handed it to him. "Fill it up, please."

"My kind of cowgirl right here." Hank winked at her and gave her a double portion.

She held the plate and glanced around. "Where do I pay for this?"

"Meals are included with your reservation, hon. Find you a seat anywhere there." He motioned toward the pavilion.

"Oh, thanks."

Before she could get to an unoccupied table, a cowboy who was seated with a woman and couple of kids stood and called her name. "Miss Jones, you're welcome to join us." He stepped over the bench he shared with a young girl and made introductions. "I'm Jesse Brandon. My wife, Laura, daughter, Anna Leigh and that's Jesse Jr."

They all greeted her at once through mouthfuls as she took a seat beside Laura.

Jesse sat back down. "We're glad you're here. We aren't quite in full swing for the season yet as I explained to Mr. Vance, but he asked me to make sure you had a *real cowboy and Indian experience,* were his exact words. He sounded like a very appreciative boss, buying you a full week getaway vacation."

A week? He paid for a whole week of this? She attempted to retrieve the shock she was feeling. "Oh...yes...Mr. Vance is a very generous boss. I've...never been outside of the city."

"Well that's good news. That's what we're all about— showing city dwellers what ranch life is like. We'll have a short trail ride starting in about an hour and a hayride later this afternoon will give you the grand tour of the area. Don't miss those."

Jesse stood and settled his black Stetson on his head. "Come on, you two," he told the kids. "Let's get you to the bus stop."

Anna Leigh and Jesse Jr both jumped up and gave their mom a quick hug as they passed behind her.

"Later, guys," Laura called after them.

Carly watched the three of them walk off together toward the ranch house and couldn't keep from smiling. All three had the same walk.

"You must be thinking about something very pleasant," Laura said and pulled her attention back to the table.

"Oh, actually I was thinking of my own family—my dad and brothers." She looked up and into the kindest eyes she thought she'd ever seen on anyone. Even her own mother didn't possess that sweetness that she saw on Mrs. Brandon. Her mom was very loving and caring, but there was something, she had no idea what to call it, on this lady's face.

"How many brothers do you have?"

"Three...all older. It was like being raised in a circus."

She laughed and took a bite of buttered biscuit. After a few seconds, "Sounds like this place. You should feel right at home, Carly. How did you like the *glorified* Indian teepee?"

Perfect description, she thought and grinned. "It was nice. I was surprised at the furnishings."

"Most of them are outfitted like that, but yours is the one we reserve for honeymooners."

"Ah...so that's why it's set off a ways by itself."

She nodded and grinned, then both women concentrated on finishing off their food.

Laura rose and gathered up her family's breakfast trash. "I see Jesse is getting horses saddled for the trail ride. Go around to the front of the barn there and he'll get you ready to go."

"Oh...I...don't—"

Laura saw her face pale slightly. "Guess you've never ridden before. Most of our trail riders are first timers. You'll love it. Jesse will take good care of you. Go on."

Carly walked straight to the bathroom cabin hoping she could think up a good excuse to get out of getting on a horse.

The thought turned all that good breakfast she just swallowed upside down. This was not part of the deal. Was it?

She exited the cabin and looked toward the barn where several horses were standing saddled and tied up. A young cowboy was helping a couple of kids—putting one girl about eight years old in the saddle and motioning at a teen boy to stand back a little ways. These were kids. Surely if *they* could ride a horse, she could survive it. But that didn't seem to relieve the mass of butterflies assaulting her stomach. She splayed her hand across her abdomen and decided to head for the cover of her teepee. Her teepee? Oh man, she had to get busy and find out who this Doss person was that lived around here and get back to the real and safe world of concrete, honking horns and tall buildings. *And*—she had a nice little piece of her mind to serve up to Mr. Webber Vance. Of all the nutty things he could ever do—to send her off to—

"Carly Jones, over here. Your ride is waiting."

The masculine voice that yelled across the ranch yard stopped her feet in their tracks along with her internal ranting. She looked up to see Jesse Brandon waving his arm at her to come there.

She'd riled herself up just enough to lose the butterflies and head to the barn. Five minutes later, she was astraddle Poncho who was slowly walking beside a bigger horse that Jesse was on. Her knuckles were white with a death grip she had on the saddle horn in front of her.

Forty minutes later, she dismounted and carefully made her way back to the teepee, her thighs feeling like they had brought the saddle with them. She laid on her back across the bed and entertained visions of strangling her P.I. boss while she moaned out loud.

But she had to admit, the scenery they rode through was nothing short of beautifully astounding. In fact, the ride on Poncho was enjoyable—not at all so scary after the first few minutes.

Then Beau's handsome face formed in her mental vison. Those deep blue eyes were boring into her own and she wondered what day-work he was doing right now.

***

CHAPTER FOUR

Beau couldn't keep a grin from spreading across his face. His hands worked without a mishap, pumping a new strand of barbed wire through the pullers and tying it off. But his mind was on the foxy little woman who he'd left asleep in his bed a few hours ago. He couldn't believe she had actually crawled under his covers beside him. But then again, he knew she would after the lights were all out. Just as he suspected—her fear of the dark was real. There was no mistaking what he'd seen in the depths of her eyes—Beautiful deep sea eyes. Whatever or *who*ever had put that fear there did a good job of it. He knew fear like that had to be painful, but this morning when he'd watched her sleeping on his pillow just before he left, he could have thanked the what or who.

That sight had haunted his vision all morning. It was a wonder the new fence he'd been stringing wasn't tied in knots. He was surprised when he realized the broken strands were all done. He barely remembered doing it.

What he did recall in mind ripping detail was the feel of Miss high class's lips when he kissed her. The warmth of her mouth mixed with the sharp coolness of the wind on his face and pack of coyotes yipping on the breeze was a combination almost too much for a cowboy to handle. He stood up and squeezed his eyes shut for a few seconds. The fresh wave of gut grabbing male hormones was nearly enough to double him over.

And just the sight of a woman, not any woman—Carly, curled up with that thick white robe awkwardly bunched up around her and sound asleep beside him, broke out a fresh grin that lifted his upper lip on one side.

"Dang, cowboy, anything you want to share, I'm all ears."

Beau jumped a foot sideways, almost landing against the new barbs he'd just run.

Andy burst out laughing, as he brought one leg up and rested it lumpishly on his saddle horn to shift the position of his cramped backside.

"Andy, you idiot. A man could get shot for less than that."

"I knew you weren't packin."

"I thought you were working the dude ranch today."

"I helped this morning early. It's too cold to swim and two groups, same family, had to cancel. So you get to look at my purty face the rest of the day."

Beau grinned and rolled his eyes. "Lord, deliver me."

He laughed again. "Okay, let's get back to that corn-fed grin smeared across your face earlier. So…what's her name?"

A deep blush colored Beau's face. He turned away, but not fast enough.

Andy's eyes popped and he was rendered speechless for a shocked moment. "Beau Doss, let me guess. You—and Ms. Jones?"

He realized Andy had instantly formed a wrong idea about him and Carly, putting her in a bad light—A false one. He shook his head and raised a hand in a *stop* gesture. "No—no, don't go getting a wrong idea. It's nothing like that. It just sort of—looks that way."

"What looks that way?" Confusion squinted his eyes.

Great! Why didn't he just run a story in the newspaper! "Last night...and this morning."

He told him the gist of what happened—Carly's fear of the dark, the coyotes, etc. "Just one of those situations where you do what you gotta do."

The humor faded out of Andy's face. "I had no idea. But I'm glad you took care of her. Mom and Dad will be proud of what you did."

"Oh, well, I'd just as soon keep that to ourselves. Things like that can get misconstrued real quick. I don't want her hurt...even unintentionally."

Andy's eyes narrowed at that last remark—*I don't want her hurt.* That had a little deeper ring to it than just helping a stranger get through a scare. "Sure thing."

Beau hurriedly loaded up his wire and tools into the bed of the ranch truck.

"Well, I better catch up with the posse." Andy stuck his foot back into the stirrup and adjusted his weight in the saddle.

"I'll catch up after I change out my ride."

50

The bumpy drive back to the barn to get his horse didn't help one bit to jar loose the picture of the little blonde girl he'd known less than twenty-four hours. He'd already kissed her— Slept in a bed beside her—Rolled on the floor with her— well, sort of—Listened to the coyote's yelp with her in the dark, wee hours of a chilly Wyoming morning. He thought she was a snob at first sight. She had him pegged as a hobo. And at this moment he could hardly wait to get back to High Point and see her, talk to her—make her feel safe.

Carly woke suddenly, surprised that she had allowed herself to fall asleep this time of day—until she remembered that she hadn't slept more than two or three good hours the night before.

When she heard knocking on her teepee door, she realized what woke her up. She stood and for a minute thought her legs had yelled out loud. "Ohh...somebody shoot me," she moaned a little louder than she realized until...

"You gonna make me use my own key to check on you, young lady."

The fog lifted off her brain then and she rushed to unlock the wood door. An older, salt and pepper haired woman stood there holding a covered dish and staring at her.

"You're Carly Jones—I'm Martha Walton." She thrust the plate towards her. "This is your lunch you missed."

"Oh, thank you. I—" She took the plate, unsure of the apparent crabbiness of the woman.

Martha bent and picked up a thermos bottle off the ground at her feet. "I didn't know what you drink, but figured hot coffee is what you needed. You missed lunch and the hay ride just left."

Carly was stunned when she realized what the lady said. Had she slept all day?

Martha stood there holding the thermos and stared at her some more. "Are you going to invite me in?"

"Of...of course, Mrs. Walton." She stepped back for her to enter. "I'm a little rum-dumb. I can't believe I slept so long."

Martha shut the door and set the coffee on the lamp table across the room. She took the plate out of Carly's hands and set it down, then immediately turned to face her. "I can believe it—after you spent the night frolicking in Mr. Beau Doss's cabin."

Fully awake and alert, she stiffened in shock and a flash of controlled anger. "Excuse me? I...I was not fro—"

"Ms Jones, you were seen running to that cabin and that's where you came from first thing this morning. Me and Hank seen you both ways. There's times we start real early around here. This morning, we started early."

Her hand flew to her open mouth. "But..."

"Let me have my say here, young lady. Then it's your turn if you want one. Now this ranch is for anybody who wants to come and join our festivities. Whole families come and singles, like yourself. We don't allow any hanky panky goings on between guests like we had here last night. There's kids visiting here and living here—namely, my grandkids. We run a morally clean place and those who won't abide by that rule, can't stay."

Carly wanted to jump in and correct what she was saying, but her voice box froze and refused to speak up in her behalf.

"Now, me and Hank, we're the only ones who seen you and it's a good thing Jesse Brandon didn't see it. You would have been shown the ranch gate and Beau right along with you."

Both stared long seconds at the other without blinking.

"Now it's your turn."

Finally, Carly looked down, then took a breath. What could she say? The truth would only sound like an excuse—albeit a highly imaginative one. The last thing she wanted was to cost Beau his job.

Then it clicked. She jerked her head up and found her visitor still looking at her and waiting. But, never mind the accusations just hurled at her. Something else she'd said. Beau—*Doss?*

"Did you say his name is Beau Doss?"

Martha's eyes rolled. "You mean you never got around to introducin yourselves? Lord All Mighty what's this world comin to?"

Torn between giving this judgmental little lady a chunk of her mind and getting more information out of her about Beau, she put her hands on her hips and sucked a deep breath to stall long enough to collect herself.

"Mrs. Walton, nothing happened between me and Beau."
She paused. The lady's expression didn't so much as twitch.
Okay—forget that. She tried again. "Is his last name Doss?"

"Yes, it is and I plan on speakin my piece to Mr. Sexy
Pants Doss before the sun sets. You best remember what I said,
young lady. Now—eat your lunch before it gets any colder."
Without hesitation, she wheeled and left.

Carly stared at the closed door and wondered what on earth
had just happened—besides a gray headed string bean in
cowboy boots blowing through her teepee, telling her that
practicing sinners aren't welcome. And Beau is the Doss she
came here to find. Her thoughts ran the gamut from Martha
Walton to Beau Doss until she sat down on the bed and tried to
think what would be the first move of a P.I at this point?

In the end, the smell of barbecue on her lunch plate got her
attention and she decided that had to be first. Eat.

Minutes later, leaning against the soft pillows on her bed,
the memory of last night gently flowed through. Beau's sweet
touch seemed to have lingered until she could still feel his hand
on her head, his fingers threading through her hair. She
squeezed her eyes shut a moment. His lips still pressed hers
until she felt the same tingling all the way to her toes. Beau—
Doss.

With a slight shake of her head, she got back to why she
was here. This should be a quick end to this investigation—
Find out what she needed to know and get back to the real
world.

Okay. She would just ask him if Leonard Doss from Sacramento, California was his father. Simple.

Except that Mr. Vance wanted this information kept secret, even from the missing son, whose name is Riley. Far cry from Beau. She didn't know his full name, but if he went by anything other than Riley, Mr. Vance surely would have given her that.

After the *telling off* she just got from the little granny, who obviously had a protective soft spot for Beau, she could hardly ask personal questions about him. Suspicion had to be kept out of her line of fire.

Maybe she should apologize to the Waltons for creating a disturbance for them last night, but it wasn't really in her heart to. She was completely innocent—it just didn't appear that way.

She shivered suddenly as a chill settled in around her. She just realized the thermostat controlled heater had kicked on. It was late afternoon, early in the day for this kind of cold. Wyoming nights were comfortably cool, but this was ridiculous. A cold blowing wind hit her in the face as she stepped out the door. *Really* cold. Low billowing rolls of dark clouds spread the sky above, growing more ominous while she watched.

She also watched as other ranch guests were busy loading suitcases into their vehicles.

Laura Brandon was coming toward her, waving. "Carly, I apologize honey, but we are having to shut down. It appears this late cold snap has unexpectedly turned into the mother of all snow storms. We're heading everyone home. Get packed up and Andy or one of the hands will get you to the airport. Your flight is leaving in two hours. We'll mail a full refund. I'm so sorry about this. It appears even our weatherman was caught off guard. By midnight our roads are predicted to be impassable."

Her eyes widened on Laura while the announcement sank in. Could she actually be this lucky! There is a God. A *good* One.

Obviously in a hurry to get everyone moving, Laura kept walking as she yelled behind herself, "Get your things, somebody will drive by and pick you up."

"I'll be ready."

In five minutes, she stood outside her teepee beside her bag and watched the entire Brandon family she had met that morning, hurrying around doing various chores. Mr. and Mrs. Walton were closing up the chuck wagon, stacking and wiping and closing every compartment around the wagon. Jesse and Laura each led horses, disappearing with them inside the big barn doors. Little Anna followed a safe distance behind them, leading a small pony. Lambs were baaing from someplace out of her sight. It appeared she was the only guest left on the place.

She stared around wishing she knew what to do to help. Half afraid of inciting Ms. Martha's wrath just by her presence, she chanced the flip side of that and headed for the chuck wagon to offer assistance.

Before she could open her mouth, Martha jerked a huge soup pot off a table at the side of the wagon and handed it off to her.

"Here, honey, you carry this one." Then she grabbed a second larger pan and headed across the yard with it. "Follow me. We'll get this food in the house and pour it up into smaller containers."

Carly followed, ecstatic that she had a part in this family's emergency. And too, that Martha was accepting her help. They worked silently and quickly, then headed back out to help Hank finish up. Martha headed back toward the house with a last stack of cooking utensils to wash.

"Thanks for your help, Carly," she yelled.

"Yes, mam. Is there anything else I can do?"

Martha walked on, but Hank looked up from his work. "Ms Jones?"

"Yes, sir?" She hurried toward him.

He pointed to the far side of the barn. "Walk around the side over there and pull open those double doors you'll see there. Just hold the farthest one open so it don't close back."

When she took off toward the barn, a couple of cowboys, plus Andy, walked quickly past her to Hank. As soon as she had the doors open, the men came around the corner pushing and guiding the wagon inside.

"Thank you, mam." A grinning young cowboy winked, then took hold of the door and bolted it closed after the rest piled out.

"Oh, hey, Ms. Jones, I'm Andy Parker." He shook her hand, nodded his hat brim and grinned. "I saw you this morning on the trail ride, but didn't get around to introducing myself.

"I'm Carly." What was it with these nodding, winking, grinning cowboys!

"Nice to meet you. Sorry you have to leave. This storm's predicted to be a doozy. If you're ready, we better head out. I'll be driving you to the airport, if that's okay with you."

"Oh, of course it is. Thank you. My bag is in front of the teepee."

"I'll get it. You hop in that red dually there beside the house. I'll be right there."

She felt disappointed. This should be the best moment of her entire trip. She climbed in—literally climbed into the dually and looked back up toward the barn. At that moment, she realized why the disappointment. Her heartbeat picked up speed and she had to hold herself inside the truck to keep from jumping out and...and...what?

What is the matter with her? She sees a cowboy riding a huge beautiful dark colored horse. It's breathing hard and prancing beneath the man who almost seems to be part of the animal the way he sits solid in the saddle like he's glued in. His hat is pulled down low on his forehead, brown hair curled around his neck at the back and half way to his shoulders. His long, lean body form sat relaxed and gently swayed from his waist almost musically with every move of the horse.

Stunned, not only at her reaction to this overwhelmingly attractive cowboy, but to the fact that she knew him. Beau Doss.

She should tell him goodbye. She should thank him for what he did for her last night. *All* night. She should hurry and ask him what his father's name is.

Andy jerked her out of her reveling indecision when he opened the back door to deposit her bag, then jumped in behind the wheel.

"Here we go." He cut his eyes over at her. "Better snap that seat belt."

As the truck engine roared and he steered a tight circle to turn around toward the gate, Carly saw Hank walk toward Beau and his horse and begin talking to him. Then, she turned and looked out of the front windshield.

She'd be home tonight and in her own safe bed. She'd be back to work tomorrow with a perfectly good reason why her mission was a bust. Or was it? She was ninety-nine percent sure Beau Doss was not Riley Doss. Beau was a total contrast in looks and way of life than the son Leonard Doss was looking for. Yes, a complete bust, not to mention a waste of her time and Web Vance's money—and all these cowgirl duds.

A stroke of bad weather luck and she was on her way home. So why was her heart hurting? Why did she want to burst out in tears?

***

CHAPTER FIVE

"Did you find that heifer and baby, Beau?" Hank walked up and gave the big bay gelding a pat on the neck.

"No, sir, I didn't, but I'll be heading back out in a few minutes. I need to put this boy up. He's too tired to go as far as I might need to. Got a hunch where to find them."

"I'm guessing Judd got all his livestock up where he wants them?"

"Nearly. All extra hands are over there now."

Beau noticed Andy was leaving out in Jesse's dually. "Where's he going? I was going to ask him to ride along with me."

"He'll be a while. He's taking Ms. Jones to catch her flight home. She's the last guest to leave."

Hank caught the flash of *oh no* on Beau's face as he jerked his head up to stare at the back end of the red truck.

"Son, I believe this gelding's got plenty enough steam left in him to catch up to that truck before it hits the highway."

Beau slowly turned his face toward Hank, wondering what the old man knew. Obviously enough, he realized when Hank winked and gestured toward the truck with his thumb. The bay didn't hesitate when he felt a spur bump his side.

Andy saw the horse and rider chasing his truck in the side mirror and stopped at the gate, a grin pulling both sides of his mouth. He threw it in park and jumped out. "Hey, cowboy, wanna trade rides with me?"

Beau stepped down and threw his reins to Andy. "Thanks, I owe you. And put him up. He's had a tough day."

"Sure thing." He wasted no time mounting up and heading for the barn.

Beau took a few seconds to shove his wrinkled red chambray shirt tighter into the back waistband of his Levis, then lifted his dusty Stetson, smoothed back his hair and repositioned it.

Carly had watched the exchange through the back glass of the truck and fought to keep her heart from pounding out loud when Beau slid under the wheel and announced in his most exaggerated cowboy drawl, "At your service, Miz Carly."

His easy smile and rugged cowboy good looks under that hat melted her from hair to toes. His dark day-old whiskers fit right in with his cocoa shaggy hair, now pulled back and tied in a ponytail on his neck. How had she missed this cowboy hunk. Everything from his bent up, dusty, straw hat to the spurs that jangled every time he moved his feet was sexy. His smile reached all the way through the twinkling long slitted blue eyes that were focused on her. She clasped her hands together in her lap to ensure they didn't reach out, grab him and embarrass her.

She smiled and twinkled back. "Well hello. This is a nice surprise. I didn't think I'd see you again before I left."

"I didn't realize everyone would be rushed out of here so fast. This storm must be a doozy."

"That's what I hear."

He glanced at the sky through the front windshield. "How long before your flight leaves?"

"A little more than two hours."

"You up for a quick side trip. There's a heifer and new calf still out there. I think I know where they are. There's a way to drive most of the way, then a short hike to check out a canyon. If we spot them, I'll call the ranch from Jackson and tell Jesse or Andy where they are. What do you think?"

Excitement exploded through the middle of her insides. "I think let's go."

He laughed aloud, seeing her eyes light up so quickly. He threw the dually in drive and drove out of the gate and down the highway about a half mile before turning onto a gravel drive and then across a cattle guard into an open pasture.

"This will take us close to the canyons where I've found strays hiding out before. It gets rough going back in here, but I rode my horse out through here one day and accidently discovered a way to drive, oh maybe a half mile from the canyons by vehicle." He glanced into the floor at her feet. "Glad you've got your boots on."

Just then the truck bounced over a rough spot and Carly's rear left the truck seat even with her seatbelt on. She grabbed the dash in front of her just before she bounced again.

"Hang on. This is a little rougher going than I expected."

Faint tire tracks across the open field had run out a ways back. They crossed several dry gullies until Beau finally stopped and parked in a copse of pine trees. "Looks like this is as far as we better go. Jesse's liable to have my hide if I tear up this rig. I was thinking I could drive farther in, but we can hike the rest of it if you're up for that." He waited for her to decide.

She couldn't stand to think a newborn calf might die out there tonight in a blizzard. "Oh, of course. We need to find that cow and her baby."

She got out and when Beau met her at the front of the truck, he grasped her hand as though it was a common occurrence and took off at a fast clip over rough ground. She kept up the pace for the most part, stumbling a couple of times. But when his hand increased the pressure on hers to help steady her, she felt her heart jerk with an emotion that felt like a swarm of butterflies were let loose in her belly.

When they exited the narrow tree line, the scenery changed instantly to barren rock and red dirt canyons that seemed to dip and curve for miles out in front of them. And they discovered, once they were out from under the trees, it had begun to snow.

They both stopped moving and stood, mesmerized by the scenery in front of them. For several long moments, neither seemed to be aware of the other—only the huge, fat snowflakes that were falling faster and thicker by the second. The brown and red earth was quickly turning white—and beautiful.

Carly was first to break the stillness. "I've never seen anything like this except in a framed picture on a wall," she whispered. "But, the picture wasn't…like this."

Beau glanced down at her, then back up to the spell binding scene. He leaned his face closer to hers and whispered, "I haven't seen snow this big and furious myself. And—why are we whispering?"

"Because noise could cause an avalanche," she retorted, still whispering.

They looked at each other and burst out laughing. He reached behind her and pulled the hood of her coat over her head. "Come on. We better get this done."

She felt the squeeze of his fingers around her hand and followed with a heart full of excitement on more than one level. The beauty of this country was getting under her skin in such a way that the thought of going home suddenly no longer appealed to her. But she didn't have a choice about that. The Brandon's had booked her a flight home and she had a job to get back to. Then, there was Beau. This lanky, hunky cowboy with a perpetual grin and dreamy eyes that had caused a grabbing sensation in her belly that she'd never felt before. She knew the highlight of this whole experience was right now. She needed to take in every second of the next hour of her life and not think about tomorrow. Only right now.

She realized then that they had stopped and Beau was staring down at her. She tilted her head back so she could see his face from beneath her fuzzy hood.

"Are you okay?" His words were soft and filled with concern.

She nodded. She was a little breathless, but she thought she was keeping up with him just fine.

"You slowed down on me. It's not much farther, but the snow is getting deep fast." He was torn momentarily between getting Carly in a bind out in this cold and the condition of the baby calf, but there was no comparison. Why was he even thinking about it? "We might better head back. This storm is already in full swing."

"How much farther?"

He pointed across a valley to the far side. "See that peak there to the right? It's just below there. This way was farther than I thought it was."

Without hesitation, she pulled his hand forward. "Let's go then. We can make that easy."

When he hesitated, she hurried forward, pulling him with her. Together they slipped and slid down snow covered slopes, holding each other up at times, laughing with sheer enjoyment of their late winter wonderland.

They reached the backside of the high peak to peer into the canyon hideout, but there was no sign of the cow or calf. What they did see was a total whiteout in front of them and behind where they'd just come from.

Beau realized with a horrible jolt that darkness would fall within minutes. After a few seconds of panic, he forced himself calm for Carly's sake. He wasn't sure what to do, knowing how easy they could get turned around in these canyons and not find their way out in the dark. It was getting colder and he knew he had made a grave mistake. He'd allowed his giddiness at playing and spending time with this beautiful young lady to cloud his common sense.

Carly had looked around and realized something wasn't right about the same time she saw the stricken expression on Beau's face. She was just hoping against hope that he would grin and begin to lead her back with all the confidence he'd had coming out here. But he didn't move. He was looking every direction as if trying to get his bearings on something.

"Beau?" She looked back toward the way they'd come and what little she could see in the near darkness was completely unfamiliar. The canyons looked different from the opposite direction. And she hadn't paid that close attention on the way out here. *Oh no!* Panic was seizing her airway. "Beau? Are we lost? Oh..."

The terror in her voice brought Beau's hands around to grasp her upper arms. "Okay, don't worry. We'll figure this out. Let me think a minute." He kept his hands around her arms hoping to keep her calm long enough to get his bearings.

He had approached this little hidden canyon looking for strays from the opposite side—riding his horse up through Judd Luke's place. It was quite a distance from that direction, but it was mostly woods and not as likely to get them turned around as these canyons would.

The wind had picked up and snow was banking up. They both had to keep their heads down to see each other. Carly's hands went to her face and he could feel her body shaking. She was crying.

Come on, Riley, think! You got her into this—you have to get her out.

He wrapped both arms around her and pulled her tightly into him. "Hey, pretty girl," he whispered against her ear, "we'll get through this and you'll have one fantastic tale to entertain your grandkids with someday."

When he felt her grab two hands full of the front of his coat, he had to swallow hard to get rid of the ridiculous lump that formed in his throat. This predicament was enough to strike fear and panic into any seasoned cowboy. He had to fight to keep his own head right now. He couldn't expect this cultured fine-china-looking little girl to not crack and go to pieces on him. He vowed silently to himself to get her through in one piece or leave this world trying.

"Listen to me, Carly." He smoothed her hair down beneath her big roomy coat hood. "We're going back a different way. I know that way better. I've got an idea, so just hang on to me. We're going down into the canyon below us."

He pulled her hood tightly forward and grabbed her hand wishing that *idea* he'd just lied about would pop into his mind real quick.

The wind was whistling now, the cold beginning to penetrate his clothes. Thank God Jesse had stuffed the heavy overcoat Carly was wearing behind his truck seat. He only had his down vest on over a long sleeve chambray work shirt. His Stetson was set tight and low on his forehead.

Beau's eyes adjusted to the darkness enough to at least see where to step and grab a hold of something as they began to descend to the valley floor. Beau was sure they were on a wildlife trail, but the snow was too deep to be sure what twists and turns were buried. He dug his boot heels in with each step and held her solidly behind him with a *killer* grip on her hand. He knew it couldn't be much farther to the bottom. So far so good.

Carefully they wound their way around a jutting boulder, squinting against blowing snow and a biting cold wind.

Beau finally stopped to check Carly out. "Are you alright?"

"Wonderful."

He thought he caught some sarcasm.

"So, what was your idea to keep us alive?"

He wanted to smile at that. At least, her quick retorts weren't frozen yet. Well not with snow, anyway. But he couldn't muster the grin that usually formed on his mouth without thinking about it. He had no *idea*—no plan, other than to keep moving.

"Come on, I'll have to show you."

Good thinking Riley Doss. Now you better get a plan before she discovers you're a big screw-up and panics!

The snow was deep when they reached the canyon floor, but relieved to have a wind break. Beau didn't let either of them enjoy that reprieve, but kept going as if he knew where he was headed. He knew the general direction to go, but they were still a long way from—anywhere.

God—what was the matter with him? He knew he was smarter than to get himself, let alone someone else, into a predicament like this. And not just *someone else,* but a young girl who had turned his world bottom side up in the space of a few hours. He'd been seriously infatuated a couple of times— once in high school and then, in college. He thought he was in love the second go around. But his heart had never tripped over its own beat like it did when he saw the tail end of that dually driving off with her a short time ago. He just prayed that he hadn't let that moment of running after her, changing the course of her time to escape this storm, cost her her life.

That thought sent a sickening pain through his belly. *Oh Jesus.* He moved as fast as he could, pulling Carly behind him. Snow was almost blinding him, ice cold on his face. *Jesus! Jesus!* This time that Name came up out of his mouth as a prayer—not as a slang exclamation like before. *Jesus, help me.*

This was all new to him. Prayer. But he knew for sure that his recent experience with Almighty God was the most real thing he'd ever been through.

Andy had told him story after story while they day worked together about times that God had helped him through tough situations. He'd told him about Jesus Christ and made him know somehow that Jesus was real—and alive. And that He could hear prayers and answer them.

One night about a month back, he'd awakened during the night to his mind remembering every bad thing he'd ever done in his life. He felt so sorry and miserable that he'd cried and begged God to forgive his sins. He finally slept hard the rest of that night and when he woke up the next morning, he felt like a new born baby on the inside. He knew God heard and forgave him. When he told Andy about it a few days later, he grabbed him in a bear hug and yelled *Praise the Lord!* Beau was too embarrassed to tell anyone else after that, but right now every cell inside his body was calling on that God. He'd never prayed before, except that one night—until now.

***

CHAPTER SIX

A sudden rise of strength shifted through his shoulders and fluttered down into his arms and legs—a physical strength that stood him up tall and more confidant that he would get Carley to safety.

With a tight grip on her hand, he tromped through deepening snow, but headed the opposite direction than what his knowledge and instincts told him. He couldn't change his direction. Even though every brain cell he possessed was screaming inside his head to go the other way, there was a compelling—a quieter push somewhere else inside him that took precedence.

Every minute, he glanced back to make sure she appeared to be all right. His strides were long and fast, but so far she was managing to keep up.

When their route abruptly became dense and heavily wooded, Carly stopped and pulled back on his hand. What little light they'd had was shut out by the trees. He stopped and took a step back to face her, thinking she was give out, but one look at the pure terror on her face reminded him. She's scared of the dark.

"Carly, I'm right here. We'll be fine. We have to keep moving."

Her mouth opened, then closed and opened again, her eyes wide. Panic had seized her.

Beau grasped her shoulders and pulled her close against him. When her arms wrapped him in a vise-like grip, he recalled the power hold she'd had on his neck on the floor of his cabin when she thought wolves were after her. He held her tight for a few seconds, then reached behind him and unclenched her arms from his ribcage.

Without giving her a chance to think about it, he grabbed her hand and took off, pulling her after him. She managed to get a grip on his shirt sleeve with her other hand, but at least her feet kept moving. He just wished he knew to where.

His eyes adjusted enough to keep from running into a tree or bush. At least, he supposed they were bushes. He was reasonably sure if one of the dark clumps was a bear, it would let him know. *Now that's a comforting thought, Riley!*

A second later, he saw it—just before he would have smashed his face into a structure of some kind. "Whoa!" He jerked free from her grip, then slapped his hand against a rough slab of wood. The sudden stop sent Carly nose first into his shoulder.

"What…where are we?" She had his other arm solidly pinched and wrapped like a sausage.

Once his eyes adjusted better, he thought the wood slab looked like a door. A door—propped against a slight rise in the ground. He grabbed the edge of it and pulled.

He patted Carly's arm. "Turn loose a minute. You'll be alright."

Surprisingly she dropped her hands and took a step back. Her eyes were fixed on the door in front of them.

With both hands along one edge of the wood panel, Beau pulled until he realized the resistance to it opening was the snow banked up along the bottom edge. With the toe of his boot, he dug into the drift and scraped several times until the bottom of the door was freed. With one hand, he slowly pulled it open.

Between the thick, falling snow and the nearly black darkness, neither could see past the framework of the doorway. Beau's first thought was a bear den, but only if there was another entrance to…whatever this literal *hole in the hillside* was. An opening with a door like this was only for a human.

"Hello?" Beau called loudly as he grasped Carly's hand and stepped inside and out of the storm. It was pitch black inside and dead quiet.

"Beau?"

He could hear fear rising in her voice, mixed with her chattering teeth. Or was it his teeth he heard? "Here." He reached behind him and guided her fingers into a belt loop of his jeans. "Hang on to that while I feel around in here. Maybe there's something we can get a fire going with."

With both hands stretched out in front of him, he took one small step after another into the interior until his knees connected with something solid, nearly flipping him forward.

"Whoa," he exclaimed and reached down to feel what he'd nearly tripped over. It felt like a bench. A few inches farther and he ran his hands across the surface of a rough wood table top. "Well I'll be dang. There's a bench and table sitting in here."

"Seriously? Is this someone's house? Maybe there's a fireplace." Excitement edged out her fear.

"Hello? Anybody in here?" Beau tried again.

There wasn't a sound, until he realized Carly wasn't pulling on his pants now, but had moved off to his left making a racket with something she had found.

Just then, a fire flared just inches beside him, sending him backward a step. Carly was holding an eight-inch-long flaming match.

"Ah, sweet. My hero!" He was shocked that she had taken steps away from him in the darkness. But not as surprised as he was at the surroundings the tiny flame of light revealed. They were standing in the center of somebody's in-ground cabin or cave. He grasped an oil lantern sitting on the edge of the table and lit up the entire single room dug-out.

Carly was stunned as her eyes travelled over the small space. A folding cot served as a bed with several blankets layered on top. The floor was solid, but warped old plywood—the same weathered sheets of wood standing upright to form a half wall around the entire room. The ceiling and upper walls were dirt and rock.

Right this minute, this crude little hut looked like the finest Inn on the continent to Carly. When she turned her attention back to Beau, she found him on his knees with a small flame started in a crude hole in the wall that served as a fireplace. His head was bowed low, his hat lying beside him on the floor.

Was he crying?

Then quickly he popped his hat back on and continued his fire building.

She glanced around and took in a few more details—like a neatly folded pair of coveralls and a brown flannel shirt stacked on the floor at the foot of the cot. Next to them were cans of various foods. She bent down and saw green beans, corn, porknbeans, several cans of cooked chicken and Vienna sausages. Closer inspection showed the food was still in date. A shallow cardboard box held a pie-tin, a tin cup, coffee grounds, paper towels—nothing more than the barest necessities.

Sensing Beau beside her, she straightened up and looked up at him, still awed by their good fortune at stumbling on this place.

"Where do you think the man is who lives here? There's plenty of good food here and those clothes." She pointed at the floor.

"I don't know, but it hasn't been long since he was here. The ashes in that fire pit are cold, but not that old. There's plenty of kindlin and chunks of wood piled there. I can't build the fire up too big in here, but it already seems to be warming up." He lightly touched her shoulder and looked down into her eyes. "You doing okay, Carly?"

She nodded, continuing to meet his gaze. What she read in those eyes melted her heart to a puddle. He was feeling ashamed and guilty that they were in this situation, but she knew it was every bit as much her fault. Maybe more so. He had wanted to head back. She pushed to keep going.

But he said he had an idea—that he would show it to her. So, he must have known this place was here.

"I'm more than okay. I might have been a little less of a whiner if you'd told me there was a place like this out here."

He swallowed and glanced away, then back at her. "Carly, I...I...are you hungry? What's in those cans that's good?"

He couldn't tell her he had no idea about this place or even where they were. Neither could he tell her he had cried out to Jesus Christ for help. In his heart, he knew it had been a miracle that they'd stumbled on to this shelter. Heat. Food. God answered his prayer. He knew it. But he couldn't make himself talk about it to her.

She held up a can. "How does chicken sound?"

"Perfect. See a can opener or any utensils laying around?"

Five minutes later, they sat on the floor with their backs to the fire and shared a pie tin of canned chicken. Beau gave her the only fork they could find while he exaggerated with smacks and slurps getting at the juice running down his fingers.

"Finger lickin good, huh?" She giggled, glad to see he'd lightened up.

"Yes, mam, it is. My compliments to the cook!" He nodded in a semblance of a bow to her.

"Why thank you, cowboy." She laughed. "You're no dummy, are you?"—still laughing.

"Nope. My mama didn't raise..." The words seemed to cut themselves off.

Her gaze lifted to meet his, catching a look that wasn't fully definable, but it was telling. She wondered fleetingly about his family—his mama—until he abruptly stood and changed the conversation.

"Looks like we're going to be bunking together tonight...again."

She stood up to find him grinning at her. He didn't know it, but that was perfectly all right by her. "Do you think we've been missed yet?"

"I kind of doubt it. That'll happen when you don't get off the plane back home. A phone call to the ranch will ...," he paused and glanced away, then back to her. "I really hate what that phone call is going to cause. Who is picking you up at the airport?"

Her mouth slowly opened as the shock of the answer to that settled in. She shook her head, eyes wide, as she locked them on Beau. "Nobody is picking me up. No one knows I'm supposed to fly home tonight."

Beau knew Jesse and Andy would assume he couldn't drive back from Jackson in this storm, but would they get concerned when he didn't call them? Would they think the phone lines were down? He knew he could hike his way out of here as soon as the storm was over, but he couldn't take a chance with Carly's life. Not again.

He wheeled around suddenly when a thought struck terror through his insides. In two steps, he was against the door, pushing with all he had.

Carly instantly realized with horror that the door could be snowed shut, trapping them indefinitely. She joined him and they finally managed to get it open enough for Beau to slip through and dig the snow out.

It was still coming down fast and hard. He grabbed the little bench beside the table and wedged it between the door and the door frame to hold it open.

"That was close," he muttered, mainly to himself. He glanced up at Carly and knew something was wrong.

"Hey." He stepped close to her and turned her by the shoulders to face him. Tears had wet her cheeks. When he pulled her tightly into his arms, she didn't resist. As both of his arms tightened around her in a way she had never been held in her life, she couldn't hold back the sobs. He didn't say a word. He just held her until she was spent and pulled back slightly.

He had to force himself to loosen his grip and let her move away. The feel of her gathered so tightly against him felt more right than any person or moment of his entire life. However, hearing her cry so desperately slammed his heart with guilt and an even more determination to get her out of here and back to safety.

Feeling ashamed, she swiped her cheeks and turned her back. "I'm sorry. I don't know where that came from."

Beau knew. She had been a real trooper through this ordeal, swallowing her fear and putting up a good front of bravery. She was a city girl. She had no clue what a coyote was and she's petrified of the dark. And thanks to him, she's snowbound in a tiny hovel, not much better than a bear den in the middle of who knows where. And nobody knows she's missing. Not yet, anyway. Whatever price he had to pay when they got out of this mess, he would owe every shred of his hide.

He stepped to her and wrapped an arm around her neck from behind, pulling her back against his chest. He whispered against the side of her face. "Don't ever be ashamed of your tears, sweet girl. Even I have to let loose sometimes. That's why Jesus gave us tears—to use when we needed to."

She closed her eyes and savored the feel of his strong muscled arm, his warm breath on her neck and face. She was surprised at his mention of Jesus. She certainly believed in God, but never thought of Him much in everyday situations, especially not whether she shed tears or not and only on the Sundays that she attended church services with her family. And that wasn't too often, since she'd moved to her own apartment. But hearing a cowboy say the name Jesus so easily was almost embarrassing. They were certainly a far cry from a church building.

"Thank you," she offered. "I'll be all right now." She patted his forearm and felt him release his hold and drop his arm.

He sucked in a deep breath, once again feeling that same discomfort at revealing his thoughts about God as he did when

Andy had reacted so intimately over learning of his experience with Him. Andy had been excited for him. Carly sounded stiff and distant. Either way, the reactions at talking about spiritual stuff made him realize that that subject was better kept private. He didn't know what made him say such a thing to her just now anyway.

"I guess we better keep this fire going and," he reached to pull the little cot closer to the flame, "you can sleep on this tonight."

Carly looked down at the rumpled and soiled blankets piled on the cot and curled up her nose. Just as she opened her mouth to object to laying on top of lord knew what, Beau reached out and jerked up the three covers and disappeared outside with them. In less than a minute, he was back and dropped them back on the cot.

"That's the best I can do. I shook them out and you'll have to use them because I'm not letting you freeze to death. I'll wrap up in one and keep the fire going while you get some sleep. That open door is going to create a big draft in here, but it's better than the alternative."

His short, matter-of-fact tone created a different kind of tension in her than she already had. It felt far worse than the fact that she was stranded in a sub-zero blizzard with no rescuers on the way. She wanted to reach for him. She wanted to feel his arms wrapped tight around her again. She didn't know what just happened, but somehow the atmosphere between them changed. Was it because she let herself fall apart? Did he see her as some immature bimbo who couldn't handle a little hardship?

Beau watched her face drop at his clipped voice. Immediately a pang of regret assaulted his heart and he stepped to her and pulled her gently against his chest.

"I'm sorry, Carly. I don't mean to take this out on you. But I've got to tell you—for somebody who doesn't possess an outdoor bone in her body, you've been a tough little trooper through this deal." He ran his hands down the back of her hair. "Fact is, if I was by myself out here, I'd probably have already sat down and bawled like a baby. I mean…if I hadn't had to be tough to keep up appearances, that is. You know…my reputation and all."

She started laughing with her face planted into his vest front. She heard him snickering above her head and knew she would never forget that sweet sound. She looked up and their eyes sparkled into each other.

He bent his head and gently pressed his lips to hers. Her response to him caused him to deepen the kiss for a few seconds before ending it, knowing full well this could head off into something he couldn't finish—Wasn't going to finish. And he already knew she wouldn't get that, if she even desired to continue what they had started.

Carly let out an unsteady breath and looked down to conceal her disappointment. Obviously, she was the only one feeling the attraction. And why she was allowing herself to do that was nothing more than ignorance. Her life was so far from the life this cowboy lived. Horses and chuck wagons and omg

Indian teepees—although that teepee was sounding *really* good about now—were differently exciting and vacation worthy. As for a daily lifestyle—not for her.

However, there was nothing saying she couldn't enjoy herself with this sweet hunky man while she's here.

She knew Beau was not shy. They were both adults calling their own shots. But not just *that*. Not for her, anyway. She felt almost desperate to be touched, to be held—Not by just anyone. Just Beau Doss.

Up on tiptoe, she wrapped both arms around his neck and kissed him, making sure he didn't mistake her intentions. "Beau, I think we should share this little cot," she whispered against his mouth.

His whole body tightened up and he took possession of her mouth again. He couldn't help himself. He knew he'd brought this on himself when he kissed her that night on his cabin porch—plus every move he'd made with her after that and right up to this moment. *Why did this have to happen now?*

His heart was pounding, his thoughts torn as though the two parts of him were waging war inside of his skin.

He'd made a promise only a few weeks ago—One he desperately did not want to break. But never in his wildest imagination did he foresee—Carly. The invitation she just gave him might be too tough to refuse.

If it was just spending a night of sex with a beautiful woman—he could step back, take a good long deep breath and, albeit reluctantly, refuse. But that wasn't even close to what it was. He'd been *there* before.

No—from the moment she had plastered him to the floor of his cabin with the force of a small hurricane, while running from a pack of woman-eating wolves, she had pulled the breath right out of him and left a fierce desire for her in its place. She was beautiful—not so graceful—and needed him desperately. Something had grabbed around his insides in that moment, even while she choked him nearly to death—even though he full well knew that anybody would have served as a savior, as scared as she was. He should just laugh this off. She reminded him a lot of his high-falooty mother and sister, anyway. Then there was the other part of her that wasn't like anyone he'd ever met—or held—or kissed.

But he'd made a promise—a serious vow to follow God's ways the best he knew how. And something was stirring inside of him, not allowing him to forget about it. He just wasn't 100% sure he could control himself—even for God.

He stepped back and rubbed his hands up and down her upper arms. "There's a right timing for everything, Carly. Tonight is the time for me to stay alert and keep a blaze burning in that pit. Somebody has been staying in here and if they happen to show up, we need to be ready for whatever."

With that, he squatted down and poked another few wood pieces into the fire, feeling like a dumb jerk.

There was no way to dodge the cold air siphoning in through the propped open door. Beau sat with his back against the cot where Carly lay curled like a snug little kitten, except he knew she wasn't all that warm. He'd wrapped two blankets around her on top of Jesse's big coat she wore, but he was still worried about her. He doubled one ragged wool blanket over and wrapped himself up.

Thankfully, there was plenty of firewood to keep a small blaze healthy.

For the first time since they'd been here, he wondered what time it was. He didn't have his watch with him and he noticed she wasn't wearing one. Had anybody discovered they were missing? It would be hell to pay for him after causing all this mess—if they even got out of here alive.

Now there's a happy thought, Riley Beaumont Doss!

***

CHAPTER SEVEN

Changing his position to take the weight off his bum leg, Kirk Colter spit his well-used chaw of Red Man out across the pristine snow.

At least the storm had let up. He figured it was well after midnight. He'd been sitting behind this tree line for a couple hours, watching for some sign that whoever had discovered his hidey-hole, was asleep. Not knowing who he was about to encounter, he figured it best to catch him totally off guard.

He pulled his fur-lined hood farther down over his bearded face. He was angry that this place was now known by another human, but perplexed at the same time. He had searched out this remote spot from all directions before choosing it to dig his cave. How in blazes did anyone, besides a bear or wild hog, happen to find it—and in a freakin blizzard at that!? Who would be out here at all, regardless of the weather?

He'd been smelling his wood burning for hours. The door propped half open to keep it from snowing the intruder in was a sure sign that whoever it was had some sense.

He jerked to attention, raising the barrel of his Remington shot gun slightly when a hooded figure suddenly emerged through the small opening in the door.

His eyes shot open wider. Was that a girl in that over-sized man's coat? He watched her glance around into the darkness. He knew she couldn't see him, but the moonlight revealed a small body that moved like a female.

Slowly she trudged through knee-deep snow until she disappeared into the dark shadow of trees. She returned after only a minute or less and went back inside.

He knew where she had gone, but he didn't know if she was the only one in there. Now, he decided, was the time to find out.

"Don't either of you move one inch or it'll be your last!"

Beau jumped to his knees from where he sat on the floor facing the fire and turned completely around in one fluid move.

Carly screamed and rolled off the cot into Beau's arms. She didn't recall moving like that, then realized Beau had jerked her to the floor in front of him. One hand was holding her to the floor, the other was extended out in front of him toward the intruder who was pointing a rifle at them.

"Okay...okay, we're not armed. We don't mean any harm," Beau quickly offered. There was a vicious edge in the man's voice and stance, sending Beau's brain into overdrive.

Kirk's eyes darted around the room, then back. "Where did you come from? Who are you?"

"Hikers, sir. This…is my wife. We were out hiking in the canyons and we got caught in the storm."

Wife! Carly looked at him like he'd just popped a third eyeball. Before she could say anything, he jabbed her in the side with his knee and pressed her even tighter to the floor with his splayed fingers.

"You live around here?" The man glared at Beau as if he was sizing up his answers.

Beau could see that he didn't totally believe him—as well as the fact that he wasn't the friendly sort. He didn't put anything past this stranger and felt he needed to be real convincing, real quick—hoping all along that he'd judged the man wrong.

"No, sir. We live in California. We're guests at the High Point Dude Ranch a few miles away. We…were actually driving back toward home, but decided to take one more hike out in this beautiful country."

"So how come there's only one coat between the two of you? Don't appear you're dressed for being outside."

"Well we're city people and it was a nice afternoon before it went to snowing." Beau laughed, attempting to ease the atmosphere between them and that rifle. "She's kind of cold natured anyway and grabbed my coat by mistake from the truck. Luckily we stumbled on to this little shelter before we both became popsicles."

The hard glare suddenly began to glint like steel. "Just what kind of truck you got, boy?"

Did the man need a vehicle or had he seen the dually?

"A Ford Dually."

"What color is it?"

"Red."

"Them plates ain't California."

Beau saw it coming almost in the same instant that the barrel of the rifle reached the side of his head with a loud crack. Then his world went black.

The scream that erupted and reverberated in circles around the small space of the dugout sounded to Carly like the pack of wild dogs she'd heard her first night at the dude ranch. She didn't realize the sound came up from her own being. She could barely breathe, her throat felt closed—her arms were wrapped around Beau. Somehow she had sat up and Beau was laying unconscious beside her. "Beau? Beau?" She could barely get above a whisper.

She jerked her head around and got her first look at the monster that filled the doorway. "Who are you?" She looked back at Beau, not sure he was alive. Then back to the stranger. "What have you done? Why?"

"Just shut up! I need to think." The man turned toward the open door as if to go out, then hesitated, seeming to be unsure of his next move.

But it was long enough. A foot-long length of firewood whirred in the air above Carly's head looking like a lightning strike and sounding like the accompanying thunder as it hit its mark against the side of the man's head. The force of the blow caused him to stiffen and drop his weapon. He staggered out the door and dropped.

Slowly, Beau sank back to sit on the floor. He could hear Carly's voice, but far away.

"Beau! Oh, God, Beau, I thought he killed you!" She grabbed his arms, then ran one hand gently along the side of his head. The lump was huge. His eyes were closed, but he winced at her touch.

"Get his rifle, Carly," he mumbled at her. Disoriented and a little sick to his stomach, he fought to stay awake. He couldn't seem to figure out exactly where they were—Or why.

Carly crawled the short space to where the rifle lay and quickly took possession of it. He appeared to be out cold. She immediately decided he'd better stay that way or he'd find himself *dead* cold. She knew it was them or him—As long as simply aiming and pulling the trigger did the job. She had never shot a gun in her life, but thankfully Beau could deal with this now.

When she turned back to him, panic seized her as she realized he was passed out again.

Jesse stared at Laura's face as she returned to the kitchen from answering the office phone. It wasn't often that he saw alarm set in her eyes the way he was seeing it now.

He finished filling his coffee cup and moved to the long center butcher block island, settling on a stool across from her. Phone calls before the crack of dawn usually spelled trouble so he waited, hoping for a wrong number or false alarm of some kind. Her face said it was more than that.

"That was Webber Vance in Sacramento. It seems that Carly Jones wasn't on her scheduled flight. And—she didn't arrive on a later one. Her cell phone goes to voice mail. And, as you know, we haven't heard from Beau."

He sat up straight and stared into space, thoughtful a few moments. "Okay, well, we figured all the options with Beau. But with phone lines still working, he should have called in. The boy takes care of business better than most." He took a long slurp of hot coffee and squinted his eyes hard into his steaming cup.

"Jesse…"

He jerked his eyes up at her.

"Martha told me that Beau and Carly had spent the night together in his cabin the one night she was here."

He cocked an eyebrow. "Why didn't you tell me this before?"

"They were already gone yesterday when she told me. I haven't had time to think about it yet."

"Well, that could shine a new light on this little disappearance. But—they could still be in trouble out there."

He stood, drained his cup and headed down the hall toward the office. "I'll get the ball rolling. Get Andy up and head him out to start feeding the barn."

Laura nodded as she watched her husband of thirteen years move with quick, long strides—A man on a mission. She could never tire of looking at him, watching his long, lanky frame as he moved to take command of whatever needed his attention. His work load on the ranch was heavy for one man, but he always found time to play with his kids or stop and chat with the dude guests. And times like now, a possible emergency, he put an extra step in his stride to handle the situation. And after all the years since she had become Mrs. Jesse Brandon, he still treated her like a new bride—like he couldn't get enough of her.

"What's going on?"

Laura tilted her head back at the sound of her oldest son entering the kitchen behind her. "Hey there, Andy. I was about to come wake you up."

She got up, headed for the coffee pot and quickly doctored up a cup with cream and sugar for him. "Here. Drink up. Dad needs you to head out and feed."

"Why the rush?" He blew across the top of his cup, then slurped a mouth full.

"Hopefully no reason, but it seems that Beau and Carly Jones never made it to the airport."

"What do you mean? Did someone call looking for her?"

"Her boss just called. Webber Vance. I'm glad I notified him of her early return. Otherwise, we wouldn't have known so quickly."

Both turned at the sound of Jesse coming down the hall. "I notified the sheriff. A chopper's been ordered to air search for the truck as soon as possible. Motels are being checked. Judd, Les and several of their hands are standing by in case we need to search horseback."

Andy set his cup down on the bar and without a word hurried to his room to dress.

Within five minutes, Jesse and Andy were geared up and stepped into boots at the back door.

Without a word spoken, Laura walked to them, made eye contact with her husband, and all three grasped hands. Jesse prayed.

At the Amen, Andy rushed out the door. Jesse glanced at his retreating back before reaching both arms out to pull his bride tightly against him.

There wasn't a spot on the face of the earth she'd rather be than snuggled in this man's muscular arms. He loved her with all he had to give of himself and he loved their children—And he loved his Lord God.

"Marry me, Mrs. Brandon."

His deep drawl in her ear made her heart skip it's next beat. How many times had he asked her that over the past thirteen years of their marriage? Dozens. One of these days, she vowed silently, she would take him up on that—again.

"I'll think about it."

"Promise?"

"Yep, soon as I get the kids up and fed and laundry done."

He kissed her hard on the mouth, then looked deep into her eyes a few seconds before going out.

She squeezed her eyes shut for a moment, sucked in a deep breath, then let it out with a sigh. At times, she felt like she was living a lie—a secret life that shouldn't be secret from Jesse. He was her knight in shining armor; the one who had taught her what real love looked and felt and tasted like. The one she would die for, if need be. But for the past years, she had lived a different kind of existence while continuing her beautiful life in every way with her husband and three children. It was all as it should be, except for the one part that Jesse couldn't understand.

Almighty God had placed a call on her life, on her time and in a unique way. The one time she had shared it with him, he'd firmly rejected what she had shown him. That was nearly two years ago. So, it remained her secret. Hers and God's.

Jesse followed Andy into the barn and began loading blocks of hay into a wheelbarrow to distribute to each stall. He pushed the loaded cart over to where Andy was scooping grain and stopped.

"So, why do I get the feeling you know something about Beau and Miss Jones?"

Andy straightened and looked at him. "Must be my lyin' face. Been meaning to work on that."

"Yeah, well, you can work on your face later. Right now, I need to know what you know."

"Nothing about their disappearance, Dad. But Beau did tell me that she ran like a scared rabbit to his cabin after he delivered her to her teepee that first night. He said she was scared to death of the dark and a pack of coyotes that started yelping. She stayed in his quarters. That's all I know."

Jesse stared into the grain bin, nodded, then continued down the isle of the barn with his load of hay. "Bin's getting low. Better fill it as soon as you get time."

"Yes, sir."

Because of the extreme weather conditions, the sheriff had advised Jesse not to form a search party from the ranch just yet—To wait until his deputies had looked for the dually in town and toward the airport first.

After chunking the last block of hay in the feeders, he sat on a small square bale against the back wall of the barn. The scent of pine shavings and horse always gave him a heavy sense of being home—His place in the world where contentment was deep and cherished.

Only his wife could top his love for his way of life on this ranch, along with their three children, of course. But even as much as he loved his kids, that was a different relationship. They would grow up and leave home, come around for visits now and then.

But Laura was his stabilizer. No one had ever made him feel like she did. He let her know that in every way he could think of. He showed her the intensity of his love for her—they had fun, they laughed a lot, cried together, made love to the extreme. She seemed to be as happy as he was. So why did she have such a need for attention that she would accept something so bazaar as believing she was getting some sort of love letters from—God.

He thought he had put a stop to her nonsense a long time ago, after she showed him a hand scribbled message that God had supposedly spoken to her, telling her to write it down.

But she didn't stop. He discovered two notebooks filled with such words under her side of the bed, while hunting for a missing sock. Endearments from God to her were on nearly every page along with sentences and phrases he couldn't understand.

Why is what he needed to know? Why was she seeking that kind of love, even from God?

This began shortly after she came close to being shot by a perverted maniac in the barn—a man who had kidnapped Reeny as a teenager and came here looking for her. Andy's life was in jeopardy that night too. She had offered herself in Andy's place. *That* he understood. Her *mama bear* always came out when any of the kids were in trouble. Maybe there was a trigger in there somewhere—One he had failed to see.

A sudden heaviness coated his heart. It crossed his mind to pray about whatever his wife was going through—To ask the Lord to help her. But the heaviness hardened into anger until he couldn't go there right now.

He straightened his back and shoulders from where he'd been slouched on the hay bale. There were more pressing things to be concerned about right now—like a couple of young people that might be in serious trouble. Hopefully not, but a good horse ride around the area wouldn't hurt his temperament any. That always seemed to be his go-to when he wanted time alone.

He saddled Rebel Man and headed down the driveway toward the main road. He wasn't particularly looking for any lost lovers or his dually. They were probably holed up in a motel snug as bugs. They were adults and not on his ranch— And none of his business.

Snow flurries blew around him as Rebel high-stepped through the deep drifts with all the gusto of a stallion that had been penned up too long. Thunder boomed loud and threatening as he realized dark clouds had rolled back in, blocking out the earlier sunlight.

Jesse kept to familiar ground. He needed the cold wind on his face—needed to feel the rocking motion of his aged, but all-man stallion between his legs. But he kept to the routine trails for Rebel's safety.

Suddenly his thoughts became filled with memories of his brother, Donny, when he was twelve years old. He could see him curled up on their mother's fresh grave, crying with inconsolable grief until Jesse could barely stand it. He had sat across the small cemetery until the wee hours of the next morning, watching and waiting for him to work through it, when Donny jerked upright and looked around as though something had startled him. When he spotted Jesse, he had jumped to his feet and run into his big brother's arms. Later, he'd told him a Voice had spoken to him to *go with Jesse.* Donny always believed it was God's Voice, and strangely enough, he didn't grieve so intently for their mom after that.

Jesse wondered if God truly spoke to his young brother that way—He believes today that he hears God's Voice often.

And now, his wife hears a Voice. And she even takes it a huge step farther and writes down, word for word, what she hears said to her.

He shook his head in disbelief as though to help seal what he *did* believe—That something—*something* was all out of kilter.

Oh, he'd had his own experiences with the Lord seeming to lead him or drop a certain *knowing* into him about something. Or he'd read a scripture from the Bible that seemed to speak straight into him. But, this thing with Laura was too much and out of control.

Love letters from God. Thus saith the Lord Jesus.

No!

***

CHAPTER EIGHT

Only vaguely aware of throbbing pain in his head, Beau struggled to clear his vision—to raise his head. His whole body felt like a concrete slab was resting on it. He desperately wanted to stop the icy cold freeze that kept slamming into his face and neck.

"Beau?" Carly leaned over him and sponged his face with a ripped-up piece of a t-shirt soaked in snow melt.

He blinked several times as she smoothed his hair back with gentle fingertips and studied his face and eyes for signs of consciousness. He'd been out for at least half an hour.

"Beau, can you hear me. Baby, please wake up. Please be alright."

He stared at her, watching the firelight dance across her beautiful face. He tried to lift his hand to touch the tears that streamed down her cheeks, but she closed her hand around his fingers.

"You're awake! Oh, Beau…just stay still. Don't get up." She watched his eyes move past her to the door. "The man…is gone. We're safe."

"Man?" he whispered past his pounding head.

She turned her head toward the closed door, then looked back at Beau's pale, pain racked face. She couldn't tell him he'd killed the man when he hit him with the firewood—even though it was self-defense.

"He left…suddenly," was all she offered, hoping he didn't press for details just yet.

As she considered the man beside her on the floor, her heart tripped with a new emotion—an agonizing desire to take his pain into herself. Never had she ever wanted to change places with anyone who was hurting—physically or emotionally.

She had covered him with both quilts and stoked the blaze in the tiny fire pit just after checking the gunman for a pulse. His eyes were closed. He didn't appear to be breathing, so she closed the door, then tended the best she could to this cowboy who, it seemed, had slid into her heart in a way she wouldn't soon get over—even if he *had* rejected her earlier.

She got up, taking about five minutes to open a can of chicken noodle soup that she found in the box and set it on a flat rock next to the blaze. With the chill off of it, she sat back down beside him. He was fully awake and watching her.

"Hey." She smiled.

"Hey."

"I brought you some chicken soup." She held up the warm can. Know what they say about chicken soup, don't ya?"

"No."

"Didn't your mom or grandma ever make you drink it when you were sick? It's the miracle food for…"

The downcast look that crossed his face stopped her words cold. She saw him fight to control whatever memory she'd invoked.

Beau's chest heaved, seeming to give him the strength to set up. "I'll drink it if it will cure this busted head." He swiped a hand across his eyes, and then reached for the can, not realizing how his arm and hand was shaking.

Carly steadied his arm with one hand, then helped him hold the can to his mouth to drink. After several big gulps, he let go and lay back on the pillow she created from the extra clothes they had found. She set the can down and tucked the covers tightly around him, up to his chin.

Realizing the fire had burned down too low, she got up and added as much as the small pit would safely hold. She wrapped Jesse's big coat tighter around her and sat back down beside Beau. With both arms wrapped tight around herself, she rocked back and forth to help fight off the shivers. Glancing at him, she caught him staring hard at her.

A second later, he threw back the quilts and gripped her arm with more strength than she thought he possessed.

"Lay here." He pulled her down with her back to him, and threw the blankets back over both of them. After adjusting the hood of her coat over her head, he pulled her into a tight spoon. "Sleep."

She drifted off almost immediately, but not before she heard his faint, sweet whisper behind her head, "Thank you for caring about me."

Laura pushed open the side door of the barn and stood inside until her eyes adjusted to the dark interior. She needed to relay a message from the sheriff.

"Jesse? Andy?"

The only sound was banging feed buckets and a snort here and there.

Back outside, she noticed that fresh hay had been piled in the outdoor part of the lamb pens. Again she yelled both names, but they weren't answering. The old ranch truck was still there, so they couldn't have gone far.

It had been snowing again for the past hour. As she looked out across the white-out camp grounds, she remembered that she had asked Andy to bring in a small load of firewood. They had central heating throughout the house, but on a cold, snowy day, Laura always enjoyed a fire in the small den area off the kitchen.

Jesse hired a construction crew to come in about a year ago, a birthday surprise for her, and take out a section of wall that had enclosed a playroom when the kids were smaller. Now it was a cozy little den with a Franklin fireplace, a TV on a wall stand and a couple of cushy loveseats—perfect for some cuddle time with her prize cowboy on late evenings after the kids were in bed.

This little room also served as her sanctuary during the wee hours of the mornings when everybody, except her and God, were asleep. It felt that way, at least. She brought a notebook and pen with her each time, not knowing when she would hear

His sweet Voice speak to her—tell her to record what He had to say. Her Heavenly Father had taught her so many things this way, had her to write things that left her speechless and at times, on her face in worship of her Lord Jesus Christ. And, there was no one she felt safe enough with to share what was happening to her. Jesse had vehemently rejected her and the writing when she excitedly tried to show it to him. If she couldn't share it with her own Godly, love-of-her-life husband—then who?

She trudged through the deepening snow to the backside of the barn where she could see the wood pile. Sure enough, Andy was loading the big wheelbarrow. She didn't see Jesse, but figured he was just about his chores out of earshot. She went back to the house to wait.

A few minutes later, Andy came through the back door with an armload of split wood and deposited it on a small rack in the utility room.

"There ya go. Nothing's too good for my favorite pie maker." He grinned as he passed by the kitchen bar and patted his mom lightly on top of her head.

She smiled. Thanks, honey. Where's Dad? I need to tell him that the sheriff called and …"

The distinct roar of a low flying helicopter stopped her words.

"…said," she continued, "to tell him *that*." She pointed to the ceiling.

They both rushed outside, while Anna Leigh and Jesse Jr. came running down the hall from their rooms and followed them out.

The police helicopter was low and circling farther away than it sounded.

"Think they know something, Mom?"

"Probably just searching. They called thirty minutes ago and said they had dispatched a helicopter. The motel search didn't come up with the truck or them."

Laura glanced down then and realized both children were standing in the snow, barefoot and without coats. "Hey, you two, back inside right now. All I need is a couple of sick kids."

They grumbled their way back toward the house. Laura turned and pointed upward. "I guess your dad can hear that for himself, wherever he's gotten to."

Andy breathed a sigh of relief when his mom hurried back inside. At least he didn't have to tell her that he'd seen his dad riding off toward the canyons earlier. Andy wasn't worried about him. Jesse knew this ground better than anybody. A few feet of snow on top of it wouldn't be hard for him to navigate safely. But his mom—she would come unhinged knowing he went out there alone.

The helicopter had moved out farther, but he could still see and hear it. He decided to get a horse saddled and ready—and wait. He hated waiting.

"What in the name of…!" Jesse pulled Rebel up abruptly at the gut tightening sight up ahead of him. His dually was snow bound in a copse of pines about one hundred yards away. He knew for sure it was his because the dent in the passenger side rear fender, where a silly colt had planted his back feet, was visible. Snow had blown in banking it several feet up the side and the top and hood was inches deep. He swallowed at the bile that rose in his throat as he rushed towards it, noting that there had been no activity around it since the storm hit the day before.

His thoughts were bouncing off each other, even as he dismounted and rushed the few steps to look inside— *something is way off here—they could have walked back to the ranch from here—They were not that far away—Beau would have known that!*

He brushed the snow away and tried the door handle, but it was frozen. He rubbed the window and cupped his hands against the pane to look into the front seat, then the back. They weren't here, but he could see Carly's travel bag.

A bucket of ice water in the face wouldn't have had a more shocking impact than finding this. As he scanned the horizon, he knew for certain they had to be… He couldn't even think it. He was forty minutes from the ranch, he reasoned. Obviously, they didn't walk out of here in that direction.

Quickly, he mounted up and headed toward the canyons, deciding to look for some sign—something. The snow was solid and deep. No tracks could be left in this mess! After a few minutes, he realized he couldn't make any headway like this.

He rode to where the ground dropped off into the canyons—a formidable place to get lost in, even in perfect weather. He gazed a moment across the vastness of the pure white dips and curves, peaks and valleys that lay out in front of him. Its beauty was only marred by the thought that two beautiful young people could be out there lost—or worse. It just didn't make sense. Why?

At the moment that he signaled Rebel Man to back up from the cliff edge, a loud roar suddenly filled the space around them. Jesse had a split second to see the helicopter that appeared from out of nowhere before Rebel shot sideways and Jesse was tumbling head over heels in the opposite direction—down the steep embankment.

After free-falling a short distance, he finally stopped with a thud that knocked the wind out of him. He lay motionless for a while, before finally sucking a good gulp of air. He was afraid to think of how broken up he might be.

If the pain that soon shot from his hip and down one leg wasn't enough, his left shoulder had to get in on the action. It didn't take him long to realize he couldn't move..

He realized quickly that this very spot could be where he took his last breath of life on the earth. He didn't feel scared of dying. He knew that he knew that a beautiful Heaven awaited him with the next breath he would take. But—he wasn't fully peaceful with the idea. First, there was Laura. Then his two youngest. Andy would make it fine. He's a man now and stable in his ability to handle the hard times. *But—But*—raw pain seized his entire body. He felt himself losing consciousness.

"Jesus, Laura and the babies you gave us needs me. They still need...me."

His pain blissfully melted into the darkness.

Judd Luke paced back and forth across his den floor. He couldn't decide if God was speaking in his heart or if his own lack of patience was acting out today.

The thought that Beau Doss might have run into trouble out in this winter storm—could be freezing to death out there, not to mention a young lady who is with him.

The young man is a natural when it comes to ranch work—riding and roping. Even though he hadn't revealed much about his background, Judd sensed an extreme loneliness in him. He'd taken a liking to Beau the first day Andy had introduced him.

The phone call from Laura Brandon a few minutes ago didn't sound good. A helicopter was searching the area, looking for signs of Jesse's truck.

Just then, Toni walked up behind him and stopped his pacing with a bear hug from behind. He put both hands on her arms that were wrapped around him and rubbed his calloused palms over her smooth thin arms. She hugged him as tight as she could squeeze his hard, muscled up middle.

He closed his eyes a moment and savored the loving embrace that gave him the strength to keep going when life got a little overwhelming—not so much with his ranch and the immense workload, but with his call to preach.

It didn't use to be this way. The ranch and ministry seemed to go hand in hand most of the time. Talking Jesus to these cowhands was never a chore and still wasn't. But lately, his growing church was demanding more and more of him.

Cowboy Church services began in his and Toni's big log house den several years ago. When the house got too small, they met in the indoor barn arena. So many people came out from Jackson Hole and even farther than that, until the barn was full to capacity. Night and day, people called needing counseling—And that was his passion, his greatest desire since God told him to open his home and preach the gospel. But he was just one man. And he was exhausted.

Did he need to sell his ranch? Was he being called to full time ministry with no other agenda?

After all his teaching about waiting and listening—allowing God time to speak—was *he* not listening now?

He didn't want to give up his ranch. He wanted his two girls to grow up here—ride horses and learn about this life he and Toni loved so much. But it wasn't about what *he* wanted and he knew that well. Maybe he wasn't trying to hear Him, in fear of His answer.

"Honey," Toni's soft voice drifted over his shoulder from where she was pressing the side of her face against his back, "maybe you should get the boys and head on over to Jesse's— just in case."

He unlocked her arms and pulled her around in front to face him. "I already alerted Les. They should have the horses loaded by now." He pulled her against him and kissed the top of her blonde head.

She raised her face up to his and studied the frown lines that were cast across his. "You look tired, Cowboy."

Judd couldn't remember the last time she had called him Cowboy. He had met Toni when she was a very young girl, who he'd nicknamed, Pigtails, when he worked for her Uncle John Baxter's horse ranch in Texas. She had only known him as Cowboy.

Many years later, she answered a bogus ad for ranch help on the Double OO in Wyoming—a joke set up by his prankster dad just before his sudden death.

Hearing that name come out of her mouth now, after all these years, made him smile—Even made his eyes tear up.

He and Toni both knew that God had used Judd's dad to bring them together. She could ride and help out in a pinch alongside him or any of their ranch hands—As well as pray the roof off the house when she wanted God's attention. And—she loved him and their girls with a love that he'd never known existed on the earth, before her.

Toni had suffered two hard deliveries to give him Abigail and Jenny. He knew above all that he'd give up the ranch *and* his ministry for his three ladies.

It had crossed his mind a couple times lately to draw plans for a real church building there on the property. He just needed to find out what exactly his Heavenly Father wanted him to do.

Toni could see a struggle on his face, not something she was used to seeing. He was always the one who was peaceful and collected, no matter the circumstances.

The sound of Judd's one ton diesel dually pulling up from the barn with a loaded horse trailer, instantly changed him into all business. He moved past her to the front foyer to retrieve his hat and heavy winter coat, then stepped back to her for a quick, hard kiss. "Hold the fort, Pigtails." He grinned at her and went out the door.

She stepped to the door and closed it behind him. *Please Lord, show my husband the way you want him to go.*

"Oh, you two just can't be trusted!" Laura playfully scolded Hank and Martha when they unexpectedly came through the back door into the kitchen. "I only called you so you'd know what was going on. How in the world did you drive in this snow?"

"You'd a just had to been there, Laura, but thank God you wasn't. Hank here is giving up his driver's license. I'll be doing the driving from now on."

Hank's mouth fell open, taken aback at his wife's quick retort. The short trip over *had* been a little hair-raising, but not enough to warrant *that!* "Dang, woman. I thought you were enjoying the ride. You sang loud—and purty, too, all the way here."

She headed straight for the coffee pot, glancing back at Hank with a calm, level expression. "I wasn't singing. I was screaming."

Laura burst out laughing. "Never a dull moment, huh, Hank?"

He chuckled as he made his way to the refrigerator to check the inventory. "How about I scare up a big pot of soup. Those boys are going to be starving when they get back here, not to mention the two renegades they're looking for."

Laura headed down the hallway to check on the kids. "Bless you both. Kitchen is all yours."

Just then, Andy cracked open the back door enough to tell his grandparents he was riding out a ways to see what he could see. "Tell mom for me. We'll be back as soon as possible."

"You be careful, young man." Martha waggled a finger toward him as he shut the door.

Andy quickly stepped up in the saddle of the ranch gelding he was leading and rode out before his mom could hear him and ask about Jesse again. He just hoped his gut feeling was off today. He couldn't shake the feeling that his dad was needing his help.

Without thinking about it, he suddenly turned and headed in the opposite direction than where he'd seen Jesse ride off. For some reason, he felt he needed to go get his Uncle Donny.

Reeny Brandon sat at the square-top log dining table and sipped at a cup of hot lemon tea with honey and toured the interior of hers and Donny's small and cozy log cabin with her eyes. She could almost see it all from where she sat, never tiring of the view. She had never grown used to her own unique spot on High Point Dude Ranch.

She and Donny had chosen the floor plan together and labored side by side, along with a crew of home builders, until the door keys were handed to them.

He had offered to build her a much larger home, but the small spaces made her feel safe. She would have been content to live in the Honeymoon Hideout forever, but that wasn't possible. It was part of the dude ranch's guest accommodations.

Jesse had deeded a ten-acre tract to Donny and her for a wedding present three years ago and six months later, they began the fun task of finding the right furnishings.

A small two-stall barn was built about twenty-five yards behind the house. Everything was pine log, including most of the furniture. The whites and tans and reds throughout in curtains, throw pillows, bed coverings—softened the wood structure, turning it into the young Brandon couple's own spot of Heaven on earth.

Reeny had welcomed Laura's and Granny Martha's finishing touches with pots of cactus and silk wild flowers strategically placed inside as well as on the tiled covered patio out back. A few rustic pieces of artwork, Indian pots and colorful woven rugs warmed her home and heart at the same time.

After taking in her surroundings one more time, she knew if it wasn't for her handsome cowboy husband, who was still asleep in their upstairs loft, none of this would mean anything to her. Donny was her life. He had been sent by Almighty God to rescue her from a horrendous life of severe abuse. She owed him her life. At least, she felt that way, even when he continuously told her to give God all that praise.

I'm just a tool He used to break you out of your cage. Don't dishonor me with the praise that belongs to Him.

It was those words that helped her put the thanks where it belonged, but she was still trying to understand the difference in praising Donny for what he did, and simply loving him more than life itself. Maybe it wasn't that big of a deal, but he seemed to think it was.

She got up, quietly went upstairs and slipped under the covers. His back was to her and she wrapped an arm around his t-shirt clad waist. It wasn't often that he slept late—or was even in the house much past six o'clock. Days on this ranch and on the neighboring Double OO usually began at daybreak.

Reeny knew that Donny had been up most of last night. He wasn't sick, but when she woke up around 1am and looked over the balcony, he was pacing back and forth across the whole downstairs.

Two hours later, she saw him on his knees beside his easy chair, hands raised in worship to God.

Finally, he had come back to bed and fell asleep almost the moment his head touched his pillow. She hoped for his sake that he got whatever answers he needed. It hurt a little that he hadn't tried to confide in her, but he loved her without question. That was enough.

The sound of a horse's whinny directly under the bedroom window brought Donny out a sound sleep. He propped up on his forearm and listened, not sure he wasn't dreaming. The answering squeal coming from his barn brought his feet to the floor.

By the time he reached the window, the visitor had moved out of sight, but deep tracks proved he had heard a horse down there.

"Who is it?" Reeny sat up, realizing she had dozed off. A glance at the bedside clock said it was almost ten—an hour later than when she laid down.

"I don't know. Some knot head out joy-riding in the snow. I'll go see." He pulled on his jeans and headed down just as a knock sounded on the front door.

Donny could see Andy through the small glass pane in the door. He swung it open as he raked his hair back with his fingers.

Andy stood silent a moment at the sight of his uncle looking like *what the cat hauled in.*

Donny grinned at the thoughts he could see on Andy's face. "Watch your mouth, kid. Come on in."

He laughed out loud. "I didn't say a word."

"Uh-huh."

"I'm holding my horse here. Just thought you needed to know what's going on." He related the information on Beau and Carly. "Dad rode out nearly two hours ago, headed toward the canyons, I think. I'm going that direction now."

"Just hold up a minute and let me get saddled."

Fifteen minutes later, the two men were mounted and headed toward the front of the property. Just as they reached the entrance gate, a posse from the Double OO drove their loaded rig in from the south at the same time that Jesse's stallion came trotting toward them from the west. His reins were flying loose and the saddle was empty.

Donny jumped down to catch Rebel before he could get into mischief with the other horses. A quick glance down his legs and sides showed he wasn't injured.

He exchanged an alarmed glance with Andy, both knowing that Jesse could control this horse with not much more than a whistle.

Judd exited the dually then and tromped over to where Donny held the riderless pony.

"Judd, have one of your boys take Rebel Man on to the barn and put him up. We need to find Jesse."

"Alright." He took his reins and started back toward the trailer. "Head on out. We'll catch up."

Donny mounted his horse and he and Andy followed the plowed trail in the snow, hoping Rebel hadn't veered off of his homebound path too far.

Within a couple of minutes, several of the Double OO hands caught up with them.

Rebel's tracks seemed to the leading away from the canyon area where Jesse should have gone.

Donny pulled up and signaled to the others to come in closer. "Andy and I will head due west. You four pair up and each follow a north and south line away from us. Don't separate from your partner. We got enough missing people to hunt for now."

He glanced at each man's loaded scabbard attached to their saddles. "Shoot once if you find anything." He nodded his hat toward them. "Thanks, boys."

He and Andy rode straight toward the canyon valley as fast as they could maneuver through the deep snow.

When they came up on Jesse's snow packed dually, it became obvious that someone had already found it. Horse tracks led up to it and the door windows had been wiped off.

"Dad must have been here. There's more tracks out there." He pointed ahead.

They rode on until finally both stopped to view the valley below them—a shimmering winter wonderland. It was perfectly still—no sound or wind. Thankfully the snowfall seemed to have ended.

"Jesse!" Donny cupped his hands and yelled. Then again. Nothing responded except his own echo. He couldn't help the twist in his gut—the sinking feeling that this was going to be a really bad day.

A new sound, off in the distance from where they had come, broke the stillness. Sirens.

Both men turned toward the wailing noise, then looked at each other.

"That could be good or bad," Donny mumbled.

Just then, a helicopter drummed in the distant sky. It grew louder within seconds and sounded like it might be landing back behind them somewhere.

"Dad's out here somewhere, Uncle Donny." He bumped his horse with a spur and headed toward the canyon rim.

The distinct sound of a helicopter was close by. Jesse stirred and fought to open his eyes. He was just cold at first. Then, he hurt—all over.

He remembered that the copter had scared Rebel and he had twisted out from under him.

Flat on his back, he slowly turned his head, one way, then the other, looking around as far as possible. Thankfully, he didn't see his horse laying anywhere. Did he make his way back to the barn? That might be his only chance of someone knowing he was out here.

The stutter of copter blades came again. It was low—not too far off. He wondered why it was flying around here, then remembered his dually stuck under mounds of snow beneath a semi-circle of pines. Beau and—the girl. He couldn't recall her name. They were searching for those kids.

"Daaad!"

He jerked and fought to clear the fog that surrounded his brain. "Andy." He had to get louder than that. "An-dy!" His face felt stiff—frozen.

Then he heard, "Dad!" Directly above him. Eyes open, he looked up into the faces of his son and brother. They were both on hands and knees, peering over the edge of the snow white cliff.

His eyes stung at the sight. He raised one hand and waggled his fingers at them. That was all he could tolerate at the moment.

"Jesse, don't try to move. There's a rescue crew out here. Don't move."

Andy had already mounted up and rode back to get help. The copter had landed in the pasture near the front gate. Two ambulances and two cars from the sheriff's department were congregated there, needing a direction from someone.

Andy gave it.

***

CHAPTER NINE

Beau kept his arm lightly around the girl who was curled up in a tight ball, trying not to disturb her sleep. He concentrated hard to recall where he was. One thing he knew for sure—it was freezing in here and his head hurt like the devil.

He squeezed his eyes shut, then opened them, hoping for clearer vision. This was some sort of cave. A lantern was on a table, dimly lighting the small space around him. He noticed the stack of firewood, then the pit of ashes.

Slowly he lifted his arm away from her, pushed the old tattered blankets off and sat up. He was shaky, but stood and waited until the room stood still again.

Within a few minutes, he had a fire blazing in the tiny pit. He stepped to the door, turned the knob and pushed, but it didn't budge. It was locked down tight. *Why?*

He turned and moved his gaze to the girl's face. His eyes creased in confusion as he fought off the panic creeping into his mind.

Think. Think.

Then he remembered. The girl had called him Beau. And she was crying.

He ran his hands through his hair and felt the lump ballooned out on one side of his head. A sharp intake of breath made him cough and the girl's eyes opened wide.

Carly sat up immediately, feeling the cold penetrate her clothing. The fire was blazing with fresh wood pieces just beginning to burn.

The room was dim, but she could see that Beau's eyes looked blank as he stared at her.

"Beau? Are you alright?" *Did he look outside and see the dead man?*

After a full minute, he finally spoke, still staring intently at her. "Why are we locked in here?"

Plainly, he wasn't good awake or he was still too weak to think straight. She stood and stepped to him.

"We're not locked in. We found this shelter when we got lost in the storm, remember?"

He glanced around the room, taking in every detail as if he'd never seen it before.

"Beau, you had a hard hit on the side of your head. Maybe you should lay back down and rest."

His gaze settled on her again. Somehow, she looked familiar. It was her eyes. He had looked into those deep green pools before. "Who are you?"

She narrowed her eyes on his, just realizing the seriousness of his head injury. He truly didn't know her.

A wave of panic washed over her, but she grabbed herself back together and held on.

"I'm Carly—Jones." She watched his expression for some sign of recognition. There was none.

"Why are we in here?"

"We—were lost in the storm and found this place," she repeated to him.

"Who locked the door?"

"It's not locked, Beau."

She stepped around him and pushed on the door. It wouldn't budge. He put both of his hands above hers on the door, but it was stuck solid.

"Oh, no." She remembered that he had propped the door open to keep the snow from banking against it, before their intruder showed up. "I forgot to prop it open."

She deliberately left out the part about a dead man laying just the other side of it.

"We're snowed in here."

Somehow that caused him to relax, even though he couldn't make clear sense of why they were out in a snow storm—or where—or why he was with her. *She had called him Beau. Where did she get that from? His name wasn't Beau.*

But he *did* have a headache from hell with nausea to go with it. The cold seemed to have reached plumb to his bones suddenly.

Carly thought he was going to pass out. She grasped him around the waist and helped him to the cot. Trembling and weak, he let himself collapse with a moan.

She snatched up the old blankets and wrapped them snug around him. "Just rest, Beau. I'll take care of you."

She turned toward the fire pit to build up the heat as much as possible when she heard him mumble something that caused her to jerk around with her mouth open.

"My name is Riley Doss."

Dumbfounded was the mild version of her next minute. She stood there and stared—at the man she had come to Wyoming to find.

He is Riley Doss? Could this be a really rare coincidence?

She studied his handsome face while he slept. He'd fallen asleep so fast, she wasn't sure he was aware that he'd told her his name.

Now, sitting on the floor beside his cot, she took in his long hair and clothes. The man was pure cowboy, right down to the worn-thin butt of his jeans. This was no preppy California rich kid, born with a silver spoon—a runaway rebellious ingrate. Beau was anything but that. Beau was—Beau.

She popped up off the floor and began pacing back and forth in the small room, stopping a moment to stare at the sleeping man on the cot. Then she paced some more.

This was Riley Doss?—The son of Leonard Doss, the tyrant, lawyer and in-general jerk? The one she had come here to find? This cowboy was, according to the owners of this ranch, a top hand—a rider and roper and apparently skilled in this way of life. And strangely enough, the Riley she had seen in the picture and was told of his background, was not someone she would be attracted to. Not her type—although she'd never actually imagined what her type would be. Not a *cowboy,* for sure.

But Beau Doss—funny, sexy, sure-of-himself Beau. She looked at his form wrapped under blankets, sleeping soundly. *That* was her type. At least her fluttering heart was telling her that she wanted to get to know him a lot better.

Everything had changed in the past couple of days. So much trauma, and yet, she couldn't seem to begrudge any of it.

Her life, since moving out of her parents' home, had quickly taken on a mundane routine—apartment to work and back to apartment. Wasn't that how life was supposed to be?

Since taking on the P.I. assignment to the wilds of Wyoming, in just three days her entire gentle world turned to play by play chaos. And oddly, she would not go back to it if she had a choice.

It dawned then—what if Beau is the Riley Doss she was sent to find? Did he want to be found? He was a man living his own life. He didn't *have* to be accountable to anyone.

It had appeared to her, after the one encounter with Leonard Doss in Mr. Vance's office, Beau probably had good reason to disappear. He had *obviously* changed his name.

But regardless of any of that, he seemed to be having trouble remembering where they were or—who she was.

"Oh, Beau," she whispered into the dim light of the cave. "Please remember me."

She got up and built up the fire, noticing their ample wood supply was beginning to dwindle. She'd have to ration it the best she could.

She was hungry. Beau more so needed to eat and drink whatever liquids she could get down him. She opened a can of chicken and chicken noodle soup and placed the cans near the fire to heat.

He began to stir. When he tried to rise up, she dropped to her knees beside him and gently pushed him back down.

"Don't get up too fast. Look, I've got chicken to eat and..."

"Water."

The three gallon jugs of water were down to two. They had agreed to ration that from the start, but she knew he needed more now.

"I'll get you some water. Let's see if you can sit up. Go slow." She put her arm around him and helped him upright. He dragged one lead-filled leg at a time off the cot. "Be still a minute until you get adjusted to sitting up."

Was she a nurse or something?

She handed him a cup of water and he downed it. Then she held the soup can up to his mouth and he took it from her. "Thanks. I can handle this."

He emptied the can, noodles and all, then reached his fingers into the can of chicken and hauled out a mouthful.

He stopped chewing suddenly and turned his head to look at her. With his mouth full, he mumbled, "Did you eat? Is there more?"

She couldn't keep the smile off her face. "Yes, there's plenty more. I'll eat later. This is all yours."

He nodded and emptied the can of chicken. She offered him another cup of water and he drank that before easing himself back down.

His head still hurt, but it was bearable. He touched the lump and tried hard to recall how it happened—and why he and this girl, Carly, were in this hole-in-the-ground and snowed in. There had to be a reasonable explanation.

But his focus was mostly on Carly. He had never had anyone wait on him like she was doing. She seemed to be genuinely concerned about him. He was always alone, even when he was sick or hungry. His mom and dad were never home. They just came and went—barely noticing that he was there.

He watched her settle herself on the floor. She was wearing a man-sized overcoat. When she glanced up to see him staring at her, her eyes smiled at him. The tenderness he saw in those eyes—eyes looking at him—was overwhelming. Why couldn't he remember who she was? This beautiful lady who treated him as if—as if she loved him. His eyes welled and he closed them against the sting of hot tears.

Immediately, he felt her soft hand smoothing his hair away from his face. Her finger lightly brushed an escaped tear off his cheek, as she kissed his forehead.

"You're going to be all right. You'll see. We'll get out of here soon."

Dear God, please let him be all right.

A thousand and one words of angry reprimand sparked in Laura's mind until she had to forcefully pray to stop the onslaught. She preferred to be mad. It felt better for the moment, but she reminded herself that Jesse could have died today. It was by a miracle of God that he was found before he froze or bled to death. All she knew at this moment was that he was conscious and his vitals were fair when they loaded him in the helicopter.

The pilot had radioed for ground help after watching a man get thrown off his horse and disappear down a steep cliff. Every rescue unit in the county was on a call and it took a couple of hours to get to High Point.

Thankfully, Andy and Donny had already found him and were able to lead rescue to him.

At least it had stopped snowing. The sun was trying to show itself, but the temperature was still below freezing.

One of the deputy sheriff's car radio crackled and voices came through in broken pieces, but he seemed to understand every word. She had graciously accepted the deputy's offer to drive her to the hospital in Jackson. Jesse's condition should be evaluated by the time she got there. Even with chains on the tires, the highway was hazardous and slow going.

Donny had flown with Jesse, while Andy brought the horses back in and broke the news to her. There was no time to think as the deputy pulled up immediately behind Andy.

Now that she could think, she had to waste time battling the onslaught of anger that Jesse would go out like that and put himself in a position to get hurt. Praying didn't feel good right now—feeding her fury did. But that wouldn't help Jesse.

"Forgive my anger, Lord. Help me. Please help Jesse," she whispered faintly with her head bowed.

She gazed out across the deep drifts banked up all along the fence line. The sun had peeked through the thick, grey clouds only a few seconds during the trip to the city.

The young deputy hadn't tried to engage her in conversation. In fact, he'd been quiet and concentrated on his driving the entire trip. She sensed that he was deliberately with-drawn—Maybe shy or just plain exhausted.

But when he pulled the patrol car up close to the emergency entrance of the hospital, it quickly became clear what the problem was. He paused in such a way that Laura could tell he had something on his mind—more than just getting her to Jesse's side at the hospital.

He didn't turn fully around to face her, but cut his eyes toward her. "Mrs. Brandon, I'm just curious. What language were you speaking a little while ago?"

A moment passed before she realized what he was talking about—then another few seconds before she could decide how to answer him. She hadn't realized that she was praying loud enough for him to hear, nor was she aware that her prayer had come out of her mouth in her undiscernible spirit language.

It was a strange thing that had happened to her while she was singing a praise song one night during her special time with the Lord. Her song began in perfectly understandable English—then changed in the middle of it to a strange sounding language she had never heard nor learned.

She had stopped singing and sat down on the edge of the loveseat feeling a serene awe at what had just happened. She knew what it was. She had read the scripture many times about

God's gift of speaking in an unknown tongue—a language that only God Himself understands. The scripture said that the Holy Spirit, who lived inside of her was giving her those strange sounding words. She had prayed and sang many times since then in this beautiful Heavenly language, but just in private where only God could hear her.

Had she let this happen in front of this man? Obviously, she did.

"I was praying for Jesse. I didn't realize I was praying out loud."

"I kind of thought it was a prayer, but in what language?"

Apparently, he wasn't going to let it go. She had become so comfortable letting God be God in her safe, solitary place, away from ridicule and rejection, that she struggled with how to answer.

"It's—an unknown language that only God understands. He gave me the words. It's—well, it's a Heavenly language."

He was staring almost blankly at her, but slightly nodded his head.

"Thank you for the ride here." She hesitated, then, "I'm sorry, I don't even know your name."

"Mick Harper." He kept his hand resting on the steering wheel.

"Mick, I'm Laura. Again, thank you." She got out and quickly went in to find Jesse.

Web Vance exited the plane and headed down the ramp just ahead of Dawson Jones.

As luck—or fate, would have it, the two men met on the jet enroute to the same destination and for the same reason.

Web had overheard the phone conversation of the young man who was sitting directly across from him.

"I'll be fine, Mom. Tell Dad I love him. At least it was a mild heart attack. Try not to worry. A blizzard up there held up the flight, but I'm on the way now. I'll find her, Mom. You know Carly—Miss Independence. Just concentrate on taking care of Dad. Van and Langley are both flying in, so you'll have plenty of company. Yes, mam, I'll call you first thing. Love you too, Mom. Bye."

When he lowered the cell phone to his lap, Web stood, then squatted down beside the young man's aisle seat and offered his hand.

"I'm Web Vance, Carly's boss. I overheard enough of your phone call to know we're headed to the same place. I take it you must be Dawson."

"Yes, sir. Have you heard anything?"

He shook his head. "No, but with the snow storm that just passed through there, communication isn't the best. Let's just keep some positive thoughts going, son."

"All I can think about right now is spanking her butt when I do find her."

Web laughed. "Or maybe you could just hug her up real tight, instead."

When tears welled suddenly in Carly's youngest brother's eyes, Web grasped his forearm and squeezed, hoping to assure him that he wasn't alone.

He returned to his seat, almost collapsing with fatigue. *I need Your Strength. Lord,* he sent silently into the heavens.

He had fought off guilt and misgivings over sending Carly off on a wild goose chase. Where was his brain? Desperation had clouded good judgement. He just prayed the outcome wasn't more than any of them could bear—allowing a beautiful, young woman to travel across the country alone. He had sent her—*pushed* her into agreeing to this when she clearly didn't want to go.

He'd prayed so intently for God to let Carly be found unharmed. He wanted to pray more, but there wasn't anymore words to say to the Almighty. He'd voiced them all more than once—silently and out loud. *Please God.*

When they approached the car rental counter, Web announced, "I'll get us a vehicle."

An hour later, with Dawson behind the wheel and a GPS for directions, they headed for High Point Dude Ranch.

Web relaxed when he saw the expert driving skill of this *kid.* "So, what do you do for a living, son?"

A quick sideways glare landed for several seconds on the older gentleman, before he jerked his attention back to the road. "My name is Dawson. Race car driver-mechanic. But, I have a question for you."

Here it comes. He knew it would.

"Okay, ask."

"Why did you send my sister out here by herself to do a job she isn't qualified for?"

He sucked a deep breath and slowly exhaled before he turned and faced his accuser. "I've asked myself that question over and over...Dawson. I don't know where to start the answer to that. It's one hundred percent lapse in sound judgement—Not thinking clearly—and it's complicated."

"Well, sir...I have a few miles to listen to this complicated story. This thing triggered a heart attack for my dad yesterday. The least you can do is give us something to justify her trip here."

Webber figured it made little difference at this point.This boy's family was in crisis in multiple ways and he was responsible for it.

Maybe it would help to unburden to this kid—this stranger, and in the long run, give him and his family what they're needing—for now.

His voice was husky—He cleared his throat and tried again.

"I have a client who is looking for his son. He's twenty-four and disappeared a few months ago. I got a lead on a name that was similar enough to his, so I asked Carly to fly out to a dude ranch in Wyoming and check this guy out. I thought it might be fun for her—Experience a different way of life...with horses and hayrides and such. It was that simple. I never thought of there being any trouble."

Anger took hold of Dawson then and he slammed his open palm on the steering wheel. "My God, are you kidding me? You've been a P.I. for how long and you never thought a young gorgeous girl might meet up with some pervert while she was snooping around asking questions—not having a clue what she was doing."

For the first time, Web felt his age, not only in body, but mind. This boy was right. His brain was performing like the 70-year-old that it was. That should have been his first thought, and not too long ago it would have been.

Dawson pulled back his anger as much as he could when he had witnessed the color completely drain from the old man's face. Without taking his eyes off the snow-packed road in front of him, his tone was dry, "And... What is the complicated part?"

Web stared out of the windshield, not noticing the white wonderland they were driving through. He had been all ready to unburden himself on this kid. He wouldn't have any emotional concern about the complicated part of his life—but he realized his story would only sound like a play for sympathy for what he'd gotten Carly into. So, he said nothing, but from the corner of his eye, he could see Dawson's eyes darting back and forth between him and the road.

Ignoring his first question, he asked a second one. "Why does the name, Web Vance, sound familiar to me? Should it?"

Web was slightly taken aback. It had been a lot of years since someone had recognized his name, but he felt sure this young boy wouldn't have a clue about that. "That all depends, I guess. Do you have any connections to rodeo, say forty to fifty years ago?"

"No, not me. But my dad was a big fan of watching it on TV a lot when I was little. He used to drag my mother to local rodeo's—buy her cowboy hats and boots just for the occasion. I went with them a few times. That was about it."

Web nodded. The boy was too young to know who Web Vance is—who he *was.*

I would imagine that Carly mentioned my name. She's worked for me for several months."

"I only recall her mentioning you once. She said she was working for a Mr. Vance. At least, I don't *think* she said your first…"

Suddenly Dawson's eyes trained wide on Web and his mouth fell open in recognition. "Oh my God—that's you! In the picture! There's a picture of a cowboy roping a calf at a rodeo—hanging in my parents living room. Your name—Web Vance—it's signed across the body of the horse." He was looking at Web like he was seeing a ghost instead of a celebrity. "I've looked at that picture all my life."

That kind of recognition would usually swell his chest—tighten his hat a little, especially in these older years of his life. But, in light of the circumstances, he couldn't get there this time.

This young man's daddy was obviously a fan from way back, keeping his autographed picture hanging in his den all these years. His five consecutive world championships, roping in rodeos from one end of the country to the other had been his entire world. But the image of his picture and name on the wall of a man who may end up, with good reason, to hate him with the same passion—filled his mouth with a bitter taste.

He looked at the floorboard through his spread knees and mentally reflected the huge picture that hung on his office wall of him in his rodeo glory, then shook his head. "It always amazes me what a small world this really is."

***

CHAPTER TEN

Andy, along with Les Kane and four cowboys from the Double OO set out on what they prayed was a search and rescue mission—Not recovery. They had regrouped, some being sent back to the ranch to begin hauling hay to livestock, the rest formed a search party and left out within thirty minutes after the copter lifted off with Jesse.

The storm had passed a few hours earlier, but the temperature was holding to below freezing.

Les demanded that his hands, Daryl and Cody, stay together and use one shot in the air if they found anything. The pair headed off into the canyons and toward the west, two others rode toward the south. Les and Andy led their mounts down in the canyon and headed in the direction they figured Beau would have gone—toward the Double OO.

All law enforcement's urgent attention had now centered on a lost five-year old on the opposite side of Jackson Hole.

The family of the child, members of Judd Luke's Cowboy Church, had called for Judd to come to their home.

After a quick prayer for help was sent, Judd left for Jackson and the rest set out for the canyons. They couldn't be sure that Beau and Carly were still in the area, but they didn't have much time to reason it out. If they were out here in this weather, they had to find them fast.

Neither Andy nor Les spoke as they slowly moved through deep snow and brush, heavy laden with its burden of white powder. This search expedition seemed almost pointless. No one, especially Beau would have struck off in this direction. It was miles through here to anywhere, even the Double OO property.

Andy pulled his horse up for the second time. Something kept niggling at his insides to turn around.

Being aware of Andy's spiritual life and the strange way God seemed to use him at times, Les stopped and watched him a few seconds. The unsure squint in his face gave Les cause to wait and find out what he was thinking.

"What's up, Andy?"

After a minute, "I don't believe they came this way, Les."

"Well…all my instincts say different. I don't know about the young lady's sense of direction, but I do know Beau Doss. None of this makes sense. That truck was mechanically fine. Why would they even be out…?" He didn't finish his question, but slapped a hand against his shotgun chaps and shook his head.

Andy knew Les's frustration. He was feeling it too, but that *something* else he felt was taking precedence in his mind..

"Let's go back. I might be wrong, but I don't believe I am."

"Alright." Les didn't argue.

Before they had backtracked ten minutes, a rifle shot echoed through the canyons. Both men jerked their heads up, looking straight ahead and simultaneously kicked their horses to move faster. The shot sounded like it had come from directly in front of them.

The snow was thick, but easier to navigate by following their own tracks.

They joined three of the four riders as they all converged just below the starting point.

"Where's Daryl?" Les calmly took charge.

Cody didn't speak for a few moments, but stared at Les, then Andy. He was barely twenty years old and was obviously shaken.

"There's...a body...frozen. He's waiting there." White faced and hands trembling, he turned his horse and headed toward a thick tree line.

They all followed single file. Andy's heart filled his throat. Cody didn't say if it was male or female and nobody asked. It was just as well because he wasn't ready to know yet. It had to be one of them—So the other would be found close by.

This was one of those times when Andy would have depended on Jesse for moral support—Calming his crisis with the right words or a large hand would settle on his shoulder. But not this time. He was about to face one of the hardest moments of his life and his dad wasn't here. He could sense that Les was trying to help fill in the void because he knew the close bond Andy and Jesse had together. But it wasn't nearly the same.

Andy sat up straighter in the saddle and squared his shoulders. He knew—It was high time he stepped fully into his man-boots. He pushed his heels down a little tighter into his stirrups in response to his own decree of *suck it up and be a man.*

At the same time, thoughts darted into his mind—a rant aimed at God Almighty for the pointless end to a life that had barely begun to be a life. He didn't know a whole lot about Beau Doss, but he'd confided just enough that Andy knew he had never had much of a family life. He'd left his home in California months ago and nobody, to this day, cared which way he went.

Andy cared. God had led him to Beau soon after he'd stepped off the Greyhound in Jackson Hole. He had felt so strongly in his spirit to go to the Burger Gettin Place that evening and when his eye fell on Beau, he knew that's who he was there for. He took him home to High Point.

The whole ranch cared. Maybe Carly Jones cared—more than cared, it had appeared. And now this. *Why, Lord*!

A tear spilled over and Andy swiped at it before anyone noticed. He rubbed the wet blur from his eyes just in time to see the form of a large body sprawled face down in the snow. The powder had been brushed off him, but the dark blue tint of the side of his face and bare hands left no room to attempt to resuscitate him.

Les dismounted and reached him first. He checked for a pulse on his neck, knowing before he did it was pointless. Further examination proved he had no ID on him.

He and Daryl turned the corpse face up. By then, all six were dismounted and circled around. A stunned moment followed. They looked from one to the other and realized none of them recognized the man. The body wasn't bloated, just frozen and large.

Relief showed on every face, even as they all realized that Beau and Carly were still missing.

Les finally spoke. "Cody, ride back to Jesse's place and call the sheriff's department from there. Tell them what you know. They'll do the rest." He was thoughtful a second. "And go ahead and tell Hank what we found. He and Martha are supposed to be there with the Brandon kids."

"Find out if there's any word on my dad, Cody," Andy added.

"Will do." He slung his leg over the saddle in one long-legged vault and spun his horse around.

"Cody, round up all available hands to come search," Les yelled to his retreating back.

Cody stuck a hand up signaling that he heard.

"Let's spread out and get to it."

Everybody rode away except Les and Andy.

Les began to look closer at the body. "Looks like he's had a pretty good blow to the side of his head."

"Think that's what killed him?" Andy moved up a little closer.

"It'll take an autopsy to say for sure, but looks like he was hit hard."

Les stood and looked around. Nothing but trees and shrubs and snow covered ground. "If Beau had fought with this man, he would have gone back toward his truck or at least toward the ranch."

"I was thinking the same thing and that worries me."

They both heard loud calls off in the distance for Beau. Then Carly.

"What I can't make sense of is this stranger being out here in this storm...or out here period, miles from anywhere. The only vehicle around is Jesse's dually that Beau and Carly were in."

The other three riders came back in. "Nothin' out there," said Daryl. "This tree line ends about half a mile out. Nobody would have kept going through that part of this canyon."

Andy nodded. "Not Beau, for sure. He knows this area nearly as good as I do.

"Well one thing's for sure. We've got to step up the search." Les lifted his black felt Stetson off of his head enough to rake his hair back with gloved fingers before replacing it and pulling his heavy coat collar up over his ears. "There's two kids out here somewhere that needs to be found."

Carly's body jerked and for a moment her mind was blank. She was sitting on the floor beside the cot where Beau was sleeping, her head resting on the edge of it.

A quick touch to his too-hot face made her heart sink. Fever. She tucked the covers tighter around him, then got up and tried the door. It was like pushing on a brick wall.

Quickly she gathered the last of the firewood pieces and tried to stir them down into the dying embers. "Oh, come on, darn it! Where are the matches?"

Darkness was covering the tiny dug-out now. The lantern fuel was nearly gone, giving barely enough light to see.

Scanning the perimeter of the cave, she hoped to come up with an idea of what to do. She couldn't tell for sure if Beau was sleeping or unconscious. He was very sick and hadn't moved a muscle since she woke up and tightened the blankets around him.

What she felt like doing was sitting down and bawling like a big baby. She fought that thought for no more than ten seconds before she noticed a ragged throw rug that was spread beneath the rickety little table holding the lantern. It was a nasty piece of rag, but it would provide a little extra warmth for Beau.

She grasped the wood handle of the lantern and carefully set it down on the floor before lifting the table and setting it aside.

When she jerked up the old woven piece of material, she stopped and squinted at the spot on the floor that was covered. A short rope was connected to the floor board—to a wider section of board than was used on the rest of the floor. *A door. That's a trap door*!

After a few seconds' hesitation, she grasped the rope and pulled. The hatch raised up easily, but after only a couple inches of an opening, she let it back down. She was suddenly afraid of what might be under the floor.

She glanced at the lantern and realized she didn't have much time left before she and Beau would be in total darkness. She swallowed the rising lump of panic and raised the door up until it leaned back enough to stay open, then held the lantern low into the opening. A staircase dropped down deeper than she could see.

A quick glance back at Beau told her she was on her own with this. He was too ill to help her.

Carefully she went down about three steps, surprised at how sturdy they were, and held the dim light beside her feet.

Her heart was in her throat, fear of what she couldn't see was trying to swallow her whole.

The light shined on only two steps at a time as she went down. Finally, she stepped onto a solid, uneven wood floor much like the one above her. With the lantern held high, she was stunned at the cellar-like room—not wide, but deep. There were a couple of plain metal boxes about the size of an attaché' case stacked off to the side of the roughly laid floor. That was it. Nothing else.

At the same instant that she stepped forward to check out the boxes, a rustling noise jerked her gaze upward. *Beau.*

Quickly she climbed back up praying the lantern would stay lit a while longer.

He was sitting up and looked up at her when the light broke through the blackness. She couldn't make out his expression, but sensed he was still confused.

"Beau? Sweetie?"

"My name's Riley. Why am I in this place? Is it dark outside?"

"I don't…know for sure. The door is still snowed shut." She felt her heart take a dive. He still didn't remember what had happened to them—or who she was.

"I think the fuel in the lantern is about gone. It's going to be black dark in here soon. I…I couldn't find the matches to restart the fire."

He stood then on wobbly legs and took the lantern from her. He picked the matches up off the floor as if he knew right where they were.

Did he remember that? A spark of hope blazed up inside of her.

Soon he had a small fire restarted before letting himself heavily sit back down on the cot.

"Here B…uh, Riley." She handed him a jug of water. "Are you hungry? I can fix…"

"No. Thanks." He turned the gallon jug up and drank what was left of it."

"There's another jug of water."

"I'm good." He felt himself sway slightly, desperately wanting to lie down and sleep. But he was also desperately wanting to know where he was and how he got here. Who was this—Carly?

Even though he had no memory of any of this, she wanted to show him what she'd discovered underneath the floor. "All right, but I found something really strange. I want you to see it. Turn your head around and look behind you. I'll hold the light on it."

When he looked, she showed him the trap door and hole in the floor.

"There's a room down there. I went down the stairs and found a couple of metal boxes...like for storage or something."

He didn't say anything, but got up and stepped to the open hole. He took the lantern from her and when he swayed toward her, she grabbed him around the waist for support.

"I'm...I'm not..." His legs buckled and he sat down hard on top of her feet, his legs dangling through the hole.

If she hadn't had a good hold on him, he would have toppled forward into the room below. She worked her feet out from under him and sat down behind him. His head was hanging down until she wasn't sure he was still conscious.

"Beau!" She jostled him with her arms tight around him. "Riley!"

Without lifting his head, he mumbled incoherently.

Suddenly her eyes widened and she jerked her head up. *What was that?* Intently she tuned her ears to the outside of the dugout, certain she had heard something. *Voices?*

Then she heard it again. It sounded like talking, but too far away to get what was being said.

Her first thought to get up and bang on the door with something was stopped cold with her second thought. *Were those voices coming here? Were they with the dead guy? Oh, no.* Her mind raced. *The boxes. They are probably coming for whatever is hidden in those metal boxes.*

"Beau…can you get up? Beau?"

He mumbled something and she urged him harder to get up. When he didn't respond, she slid herself off the edge of the floor and onto the steps.

"Come on, cowboy. We have to do something if it's all wrong."

With every shred of strength she had, she pulled him down with her, trying to steady him on his feet on a step.

The movement must have roused him enough to half stand on his legs.

She managed to get him to step down to the floor before he fell to his knees.

Quickly she retrieved the lantern and set it on the bottom step, then raced back up to grab an arm-load of bedding.

Beau was on his hands and knees, too weak to get up. She wasn't sure he was fully conscious.

Next, she grabbed up the boxes by their handles, surprised they were light enough for her to carry one in each hand, and set them on the cot upstairs in plain sight—Hoping whoever would not feel a need to look in the hole in the floor.

She grabbed the rifle from underneath the cot, jumped down on the stairs and managed to pull the little table by a leg almost over one end of the trap door before letting it fall shut.

To say it was cold, was putting it mildly. With teeth chattering, she spread the thinner blanket on the floor and managed to get Beau on his side on top of it. She wrapped the rest snug around him and scooted up against his back to help warm him.

The rifle lay beside her ready for action if anyone pulled open the trap door. Well—action, meaning she could quickly lift it up and point it. After that it was a guess that she prayed she didn't have to figure out.

Then it happened. The lantern flickered a couple times and went out.

She wrapped an arm around Beau and put her face flat into his fevered back. *God? God? Are you there—somewhere? If you are, please, please help us.*

Web and Dawson had arrived at High Point headquarters just in time to hear the full story from Cody.

Hank was already moving toward the back door to pull his boots on and grab his hat and coat while hearing the last of the details. "Martha, hun, go call the Luke's place and tell them we need all available hands asap. Meet us at the front gate up there."

"I'll come, too." Dawson stepped toward Hank.

"Can you ride, son?"

He looked confused. "A...horse?"

"That's the only way to get to where we're going."

"I've never been on a horse."

"Then you best stay here."

"If you've got an extra horse, I'll go with you," Web volunteered.

Hank sized up the older man, figuring him to be around his own age. Going into some rough country. How good a rider are you?"

Before he could answer, Dawson helped him out. "One of the best there is on a horse."

Hank looked up at Dawson and back to Web, who didn't so much as blink. "Come on out to the barn then. I'll get you a mount."

By the time Cody led Hank and Web into the canyon area where the others had been, ten more riders filed in close behind them.

"Everybody spread out," Hank yelled. "Ride with a partner." He saw that every rider except Webber Vance had a rifle holstered on his saddle. "One shot in the air, men. Be safe out here. Mr. Vance, you can ride with me."

"All right. Most call me Web."

Hank nodded towards him and moved off in a westerly direction.

The sound of Carly's name and then, Beau's was echoing from all directions. Web felt like his gut had a large fist buried in it at the sound of those two names ringing through the frozen wilderness around him. The thickness of the leather gloves and heavy winter jacket Hank had supplied him couldn't keep out the chill in his heart. He couldn't help but believe this whole horrible situation was his fault. And from all he'd been told and the frigid scene surrounding him, this outcome couldn't possibly be a good one. He very well may be responsible for the death of these two young people—one of them, his own son.

***

CHAPTER ELEVEN

Web rubbed his gloved hand up and down his face trying to distract the lump in his throat from wetting his cheeks. He swallowed hard a couple of times, not sure he was going to succeed—his health, his age—the bombshell Charlotte Doss had hit him with many years later than she should have. But then again, she could have kept the secret for herself and *never* let him know about Riley.

He was a grown man now and had done this disappearing act before Charlotte came to him, medical documents in hand, proving Riley Beaumont Doss was his biological son.

He'd met Charlotte when she plopped down on a barstool next to his one Saturday night. He literally fell in love with the dark-haired beauty, but found out two months later that he had only been a rebound, punch in the face for the one she truly loved. Obviously, she had gone straight from his bed to Doss's according to the birth record.

Nine months after she moved out of his apartment, she had given birth to twins. By then, she was married to Leonard Doss and living the life of the rich. That's one thing he felt thankful for—his son never lacked for anything growing up.

Never in his life had he ever heard of what Charlotte had claimed when she showed up in his office that day. It took some intensive investigating for medical facts and a few long nights walking the floor before finally *knowing* that he was the father of Riley—but not his twin sister, Julie. Her biological father was Leonard Doss.

At one point, it was thought Julie needed a kidney donor when she and Riley were teens. Through testing for a match, at Riley's insistence, the discovery was made. The facts were hushed up—until Charlotte came to see him weeks before Leonard showed up in his office, throwing his weight and money around, demanding he find the boy.

For the first time, Web wondered if Leonard had discovered the truth. Did he know Riley was not his? Did he know who Webber Vance was?

Web shifted his weight to reposition the saddle more centered. He and Hank had ridden in silence, studied the ground around them and listened intently after the names of Carly and Beau reverberated through the trees and canyons.

This could have all been avoided if he'd checked the Greyhound records for a Riley Beaumont Doss *before* sending Carly on this trip. He'd learned Riley had bought a ticket to Jackson Hole the day after Carley's flight to Wyoming. He *knew* this Doss was his son.

It was clear from the start that no one at this ranch knew his son by any other name than *Beau*. He had changed his first name from Riley. Web wondered how he would react to a different last name. He just prayed to God he was *able* to react to it.

When Hank's gelding stopped suddenly, Web's automatically did the same. Both men stayed still when their eyes simultaneously spied a young, lanky cowboy bent forward over his saddle cantle and not moving.

Hank put his hand up to silence his partner. He recognized Andy right off and sensed he was fully engaged in prayer. Les was standing beside his horse about fifty yards farther up, holding his Stetson down by his side.

Web's first impression sent his heart into over-drive. They must have found them—or one of them. The somber scene made him sway slightly and curse the cancer that had weakened his body and sucked the strength out of him. He swallowed at the nausea and remained still.

Finally, Andy rose up straight, swiped at his face and motioned for Les to come.

Les plopped his hat on and stepped up on his sorrel gelding.

Hank moved forward. "Andy, know anything more than that deceased stranger back there?"

Andy twisted around. ""Hey there, Gramps."

When the three came in and encircled Andy, they were all aware of the tear streaks on his face.

"Not really, Gramps. How's Dad?"

Hank bobbed his head up and down. "Gonna be fine. Broke a leg. That's the worst of it."

Andy glanced over at the new face.

"Oh, this here's Web Vance, Miss Jones's boss from California. He and her brother, Dawson Jones, arrived a couple hours ago."

Andy squinted at Web for a few seconds, then he nodded and focused back on Les.

"I saw something, Les, but had to be my imagination."

"Well let's hear it. You never know about you. The Spirit of God didn't fall all over you just now for nothing. We *did* pray at the start for His help."

"Well…I saw a vision of the dead man back there, but he wasn't dead. He was opening a door…like a regular door on a house and went inside."

"That it? No other details?"

"No, that was all. I saw the man do that three times in a row before the vision stopped." Andy jerked his head up and stared blankly a few seconds. "No, wait. There were trees and snow around the door. It seemed like this area, but I know there's not a house or cabin in these parts."

No one spoke for a half a minute—all but one were contemplating the vision Andy just experienced. The one, Web Vance, wondered what had happened to the *cowboys* he used to hang with. This bunch of Sunday School pony riders might should have stayed at home with the women folk.

"We need to go back to where the body is. We missed something—maybe need to find out who he is and where he lives." Andy shrugged and waved his hand in the air. "I don't know. I just...don't know." He turned his horse around and headed back.

The others followed.

Andy could tell that Web didn't care much for what he'd just witnessed. But he was getting used to those *omg looks* after his few short years of spending time in prayer with God and learning to listen for Him in case He had something to say.

Today, He certainly did say something—or show something. He was going to have to follow what he felt in his heart now and hopefully this ending would be a good one. At least, he was hopeful now. And he saw hope spring up in Les's eyes as well after hearing the vision.

It still amazed Andy the way God showed up at times. All of a sudden, he hadn't been able to even sit up straight in his saddle—he had begun to weep with a strange hurting feeling in his insides—not like a physical pain, but sort of like an intense grieving. Les even seemed to have an understanding about it and gave him space and respect. Then the vision came—And just as suddenly as it all had started, it stopped.

His mom, Laura, had taught him how to pray—To truly pray and seek after his Heavenly Father. She had once claimed to be an atheist, but witnessing a miracle take place right here at High Point Ranch over a decade ago, had changed her into a true believer—a radical believer.

But it was his step-dad, Jesse Brandon, who first unknowingly introduced him to prayer. Andy had seen Jesse on his knees in the barn many times—heard him praying with his head bowed. That's a scene he copied behind his own closed bedroom door when he was five years old. And now, look what it's gotten him—eye rolls and omg looks—and a life with God he wouldn't trade for all the gold in California.

They reached the area where the body lay and stopped short of seeing it.

Andy swung his arm out in front of him. "Well, I don't know what we're looking for—a tree house, a hole in the ground, none of the above?"

He rode on, scanning the area like he was searching for a gold nugget. *Nothing, Lord. There's nothing here.* Frustration was rising in his chest, but he continued on.

Web dismounted and led his horse into a heavily wooded area several hundred yards from where he passed by the frozen corpse. The others hung back or moved in different directions. He had kept his distance from the body in case there was any evidence not already compromised around it, but mostly his focus was on the dense woods that now closed in around him.

Carefully he picked the easiest way through to protect his horse's feet and legs. One more glance back told him he and this big leggy boy were on their own, but the torn up snowy ground just ahead of them said others had already rode through here.

Regardless, he had an urge to go this way, but that business of a God-vision and trying to follow a leader you can't see and don't know what the *imagined* picture was even saying— Sounded to him like some sort of cult bull hockey.

He was angry without knowing exactly why. The scene he had just witnessed with that young cowboy, Andy, and his misguided, over-worked imagination was part of it. It was more laughable than anything else, but his boy's life, along with a young woman who he was responsible for her even being in this country, was at stake—And this group of yahoos were playing churchy games of some kind.

Yes, he believed in God, but God wasn't down here doing—whatever *that* was!

A large snow-packed tree limb cracked and fell heavily from a rise he could barely see through the trees. When it hit the bottom, it sounded like a bomb exploding. His horse stiffened and looked out with ears perked, but quickly relaxed again. *Solid little pony,* he thought and ran his gloved hand down his white blazed face.

He walked closer in to the hill where the limb had bounced off of and crash landed. Immediately his senses were on full alert when he thought he'd caught a faint whiff of burning wood. He sniffed the air, turning all directions. He didn't believe for a second that he'd imagined it, but he couldn't catch the scent again.

He continued through the dense thicket until he reached the base of the rise. There was a lot of snow, but it had banked up heavily against the hillside where the north wind had blown hard during the storm.

Then he smelled smoke again—Faint, but wood burning smoke. He looked straight upward at the rise of the ground and that's when he saw it.

"What the…"

Flat against the side of the hill was the top edge of what appeared to be a slab of old wood stuck up there above the heavy snow bank. It seemed to be held there by the snow that had blown against it.

Just as he stepped closer in where he could reach up and touch the wood slab, a faint curl of smoke swirled in a downdraft right into his face.

"My God…" He dropped the bridle reins and with both hands began to smear his gloves across the wood and raked at the snow, across, then downward. When it became obvious that there was an actual framed-in door under the snow, his digging became frantic.

Even as he finished unpacking the snow bank, the question formed in his mind— *Is this Andy's door? This has to be that!*

He pulled Hank's glock from his coat pocket, holding it at low ready with his trigger finger indexed. He reached for the door handle and pulled the door open slowly.

Where light streamed in from the open doorway, Web could see a rustic little table in the middle of the floor. A couple of card board boxes set farther in on the floor.

"Hello?"

He stepped inside where a few embers sparked in a tiny hole that seemed to serve as a fireplace—A folding cot stretched out in front of it. Metal boxes of some sort were stacked on the cot.

What in blue blazes is this? Somebody built that fire! There was no window nor other door. This was no more than a hole in the ground. But somebody had half covered the ground and part way up the wall with a few boards.

He squatted down and picked up an empty soup can—chicken noodle. He smelled inside the can, shocked that it was fresh. A gallon jug had held water and not long ago.

This had to be where the deceased man lived. But the embers were still hot and they said the man had to have been dead several hours. Wasn't adding up.

He stepped back outside, glad to see his horse was trained to ground tie. He picked up the reins because of the close range and fired off one shot in the air. The horse didn't move a muscle.

Strangely, a wave of nostalgia wafted through him as he stood there with this handsome obedient pony and this glorified rabbit hole for shelter. This would have been his idea of a great get-away back in his hay-day.

He heard the shouts before he saw the riders as they picked their way through the trees and deep powder.

He stepped back inside. He was missing something. A big something. The way that door was snowed shut, there had to be another way in and out of here.

He moved along the wall, running his hands up and down, pushing and pounding. Solid! He studied the dirt and rock ceiling.

Hank was the next inside. He stood still, shocked, and eyed the perimeter of the hole that had been chiseled into the rocky ground. "What in the name of the Almighty is this?"

Andy rushed through the doorway and nearly slammed into Hank's back. There was a long minute of silence as the three men stood gazing around, even their thoughts shut down.

Web faced the others. "That door was snowed shut. It was hidden by a snow bank, except for the top rim. Couldn't be opened from the inside. Hot coals are in that hole there and that body out there, as I understand, is hours dead. There's no other way out of here. What am I missing?"

Hank eyed Web, recognizing the law enforcement way he was talking—more like an investigator, he was guessing.

Web turned around then and suddenly yelled, "Car...ly! Beau!"

Dead silence answered.

Again, he yelled, "Car...ly!"

In the seconds of quiet before he could repeat Beau's name, a muffled whimpering cry was heard.

Hearts began pounding, eyes went wide on each other.

Web held up his hand for silence.

"Carly! Where are you?"

Silence.

"Make some noise, Carly!"

A louder cry came then and every eye looked at the floor.

Andy grabbed the table and knocked it over. The slender piece of rope became visible and within seconds the two-foot-wide trap door was open.

Hank saw the rifle barrel pointed straight up into their faces and pushed Andy into Web with such force it knocked them both against the wall. Neither of them could speak through their shock. Hank's momentum squashed the two of them.

"There's a rifle pointed straight up at us."

Web pushed past them, lay on his stomach and gingerly peeped down the stairway. The rifle was still pointed upward. He could see Carly was holding it. "Carly, lay the rifle down. Can you do that? It's Web Vance."

She didn't move it. He could see a body lying beside her covered up in blankets and not moving. His heart pounded and hurt at what he was afraid they were about to find.

"Carly—honey, its Web Vance. I'm coming down there to help you." He couldn't tell if she knew him or not, but he stepped down on sturdy steps and eased his way down.

When he reached the floor, Carly was looking at him, her eyes wide with pure fear, her mouth wide open in hysteria.

She knew him, but he recognized that fear had her frozen. Her finger was not on the trigger, so he pushed the barrel down and pried open her fingers on both her hands. Once he had the weapon secured, she cried out and reached for him, those large panicked eyes tearing his heart out. He sat on the floor in front of her and pulled her into a tight embrace. She broke into loud sobs—the most gut wrenching sound he'd ever heard.

When his gaze went to the one under the blankets, Hank, Andy and Les Kane were surrounding him.

By the time the cowboys who were searching were all accounted for, several sets of hands had lifted a semi-conscious Beau up the stairs and out into some fresh air.

Carly had calmed down and drank her fill of water from a canteen on Hank's saddle. She was helped up behind Hank on his horse for the ride back to High Point. She still wore Jesse's big coat, and Hank covered her hands with his when she wrapped both arms around his middle and held on for dear life.

When Web was adamite about taking charge of Beau, glances were exchanged, but none protested. At his insistence, they hoisted the young cowboy into Web's saddle, then watched the aged man step up and sling his leg across the horse's rump like a seasoned rider. He wrapped an arm tight around Beau's middle and positioned his head back onto his shoulder.

Andy and Les exchanged questioning glances before mounting up and riding on each side of Web and Beau where it was possible.

No one attempted to ask Carly any questions and her only concern was for Beau's condition. There would be plenty of time for finding out what happened later.

Hank suggested they leave the dwelling just as it was for the sheriff to see. The two metal boxes stacked on the cot were empty and there didn't seem to be anything else there that couldn't wait.

Cody had been sent on ahead to relay the news that Beau and Carly had been found and to call for a medivac copter for Beau. It was clear he had a large lump on his head similar to the dead stranger's head injury.

Les was a veterinarian, not a people doc, but he knew the lump on Beau's head was serious. The whole right side of his head and face was swollen.

It had been many years, but Hank's police training instincts were kicking through the ranch cook's demeanor.

Everything about Web Vance's actions spoke law enforcement—his quick attention to details like the fresh opened can of soup and being careful not to move anything that could be evidence for the sheriff.

But it was the man's actions toward Beau Doss that raised the most questions. After he had gotten Miss Jones calmed down and stable, all his attention turned to Beau, to the exclusion of everyone else's offers and attempts to help in carrying him up to where medivac was hopefully waiting.

It was over an hour's ride to the trail leading up out of the canyons. Just as they topped the last crest, they all heard the whirr of the copter circling for a safe landing spot.

Web lifted his reins to signal his mount to step a little faster. "Hear that, Riley," he asked against the side of Beau's head? "Your ride to the hospital is here, son. You're going to be good as new—feeling better real quick."

Beau rolled his head from side to side and groaned.

Andy and Les heard Web call Beau, *Riley,* and then, *son,* his voice too emotional to ignore. The two out-riders exchanged a worried, questioning glance—Andy vowing to watch out for his ranch buddy and friend with this strange man. He was Carly's boss, but seemed to be overly concerned with a young man he didn't even know.

Webber Vance was savoring the few minutes he had to hold his boy in his arms. Riley knew nothing about him, he knew, and probably wouldn't remember this ride through the snowy wilderness—Or ever know how this old cowboy's heart had cracked in two at the sight of a carbon copy of his own eyes and nose on the young face lying unconscious in that hovel prison.

He might never wake up. If he did survive, he might despise and blame Web for the circumstances. For any number of reasons, this might be the only moments he could be Riley's dad. This was his only son—His only child. At seventy years old, sick and dying, he had been deprived of him until this moment.

Tears gathered in the old cowboy's eyes and he tightened his grip a little bit more around his unconscious boy—*His* boy.

***

CHAPTER TWELVE

Web Vance dozed as he became more accustomed to the beeping sound in the hospital ICU. He had kept a vigil beside his son's bed throughout the night, leaving only long enough to let Carly and then Andy take a turn sitting with him for a few minutes. They arrived in the early morning hours.

He told the hospital personnel that Riley Beaumont Doss was his son and no one questioned it. It wouldn't take much more than a glance to see that they were related.

The prognosis for Riley was not good at this point. The doctor in the ER simply told him to contact whoever he needed to and prepare for the worst. They didn't expect him to pull through.

Web didn't tell anyone that news, but he could see there was a lot that he needed to explain to Carly. It was obvious that something happened between her and Riley. Her heart was broken for him—She had taken his hand and touched her forehead to his and whispered through her sobs not to leave her.

She loved him, too.

When Andy showed up again in the doorway, he stared hard at Web, questions burning in his eyes.

"Are you Web Vance, the World Champion roper?"

That wasn't the question he expected and it caught him off-guard. He stared back for several seconds to let his thoughts switch gears.

"Yes, Andy, I am."

"Are you really Beau's father?"

More surprise. He nodded his head. "Yes. I'm that, too."

It took him a long minute with his eyes fixed on Web before he walked over to him and held his hand out. They shook hands.

"Glad to meet you, Mr. Vance."

"My pleasure, Andy." Web hesitated a few seconds. "Is Carly in the waiting area?"

"She is. I got her a coke and sandwich. My granny tried to get her to eat before we left, but I think she's too worried about Beau."

He looked over at Beau hooked up to weird machines, tubes running everywhere. Without taking his eyes off him, he asked, "Do you know that he's one of the best ropers we've ever had work for us? Said he'd never been on a horse or held a rope before coming to Wyoming. He's been here less than a year."

This was news to Web and he knew that was more of a question than a statement. But questions were now popping in *his* mind. Web had been riding and roping since he was five years old. He'd taken to it like he was born already knowing how. Obviously, he possessed a gift for it, even though he'd never looked at it that way. It sounded like he'd passed that ability on to Beau. And now—

Web clasped his hands between his spread knees and hung his head. He needed to call his boy's mother. He needed to talk to Carly—tell her the truth about this situation he'd involved her in. Andy and his family deserved something from him, too. He didn't know where to start. Finally, he decided and stood up.

"I need to visit with Carly. I'll let you sit here a while now, if you don't mind.

The emotion in the old cowboy's voice pulled on Andy's heartstrings. It was apparent that he wasn't in good health, but there was a heavy burden weighing down his mind. Andy could almost feel the man's pain. He swallowed hard and nodded as Web half hobbled out of the room.

Carly looked up to see Web coming towards her, looking older than she'd ever seen him. She straightened her shoulders stiffly. "Beau?"

"He's holding his own, honey. Something I want to tell you." He sat down in an arm chair beside her. It took him a minute to figure out where to start.

"Carly," he looked her in the eyes, "Riley Beaumont Doss is my son. Beau, to you."

It took a few seconds for that to register before her eyes widened with surprise.

"First of all," he continuted, "I owe you an apology. I sincerely apologize for involving you in my personal business. Sending you up here alone to do my job is unforgivable. I nearly got you killed...and Ri...Beau."

"So, you knew all along Beau was the one you were looking for?"

"No, I didn't. I was just desperate to rule him out if it wasn't him. The information I got on him matched his profile the closest. Then, the day after you left, I found out he had bought a ticket to Jackson Hole. I knew then it was him. I sent you here because I couldn't come myself. I have cancer. I was scheduled to check into a clinic for treatment the night after you left to come here. Everything happened at once."

One hand went to her mouth, the other reached to grasp his forearm. "I'm...so sorry, Mr. Vance." Her eyes teared up. "I had no idea."

"I know you didn't, sweetheart. I should have handled things better. The old 20-20 thing, you know."

"How...far is...?"

"How bad is the cancer? They discovered it was too far gone to treat now. Pancreas."

"Oh..." Tears escaped this time and dripped onto her cheeks.

He patted her hand, then held it with both of his big strong ones. "I've had a good run, Carly. No complaints—except maybe one." He stared at the floor a moment, then back at her. "I never knew I had a child in this world—until a few weeks ago."

"Weeks?"

"His mother came to my office and dropped the bombshell because he was missing and she wanted to find him. I checked out the paperwork she handed me—DNA proof that one of her children from a set of twins belonged to me. The other baby was a girl. She had Leonard Doss's blood."

Carly's face froze in shock. She took her hand from his and sat fully back in her chair.

Web was quiet, allowing her time to get past the jolt.

"Wow. I...didn't know such a thing was possible."

A slight smile lifted his face. "Kind of rare, I hear."

"So he doesn't know about you, does he?"

Web shook his head and glanced away. He was quiet for a time, then cleared his throat.

She cut her eyes over at him, waiting, knowing he had more to say.

"Did, um, I get a wrong idea or is there something more than just friends between you and Beau? I know it's none of my business—at all—but I have good reason for asking."

"We haven't known each other a full week. We...I..." A pang hit her heart suddenly. Every short moment she had spent with Beau since she'd first laid eyes on him waved through her mind all at once. Never had she felt such an ache—her chest felt like it might explode. She sucked a deep breath and felt a huge lump fill her throat. This wave of emotion took her by surprise. She wasn't sure where to put it.

But she did know one thing for sure. Tears spilled over and she could only nod her head in answer to his question.

"Carly, I happen to believe in love at first sight. Happens every day. Is that what happened?"

After a slight hesitation, she shook her head. "No, it didn't—Not even close. But that second sighting was a knock out." She hiccupped, then laughed.

Web grinned at her.

"I don't know how to lose him, Web. I love him. But..."

"But...he doesn't love you back?"

"He doesn't remember who I am or that he calls himself Beau. He only remembers that he's Riley and he didn't know how he got in that cave. He doesn't remember me." She splayed her fingers across her chest and dropped her head.

"The type of head injury he has, Carly, can cause amnesia. Lets give him time to heal and get back to today. He's a real sick young man right now. These things are most always temporary."

She closed her eyes a second and prayed he was right.

Laura had finally managed to get her household settled in—the kids in bed, Jesse pain-pilled up and comfortable. At least they were all home under one roof.

Hank filled her and Jesse and Martha in on the past couple of days, at least as far as he knew about. A strange man's body was found out there, but up to now, no one had a clue who he was or where he came from.

After the sheriff and one of his investigators finished their business, the body was zipped into a body bag and pulled on a travois that Les and Hank had rigged up to bring him out of the canyon for transport to Jackson.

As soon as Carly Jones had showered and swallowed a few sips of coffee at the Brandon's home, she and Andy left for the hospital to be with Beau. They had already left when the sheriff came by to get a statement from her—Said he'd catch up with them at the hospital.

Laura had never seen Jesse in such a foul state after hearing Hank's story. Holding that cowboy down with a broken leg under normal circumstances would have been a tough chore, but with all that had happened, he was impossible, now that he knew about it.

But his pain meds had time to kick in and make him drowsy by the time the kids left for the hospital—promising to call as soon as they got there and knew Beau's condition.

Hank and Martha left for home and Laura took a smoking cup of decaf coffee to her den lounge chair and soaked in the quietness of the late night.

And it *was* quiet—peaceful. So much so that she set her coffee down and praised God, letting the *sweet peace that surpasses understanding,* as the Bible calls it, permeate her fully.

In the midst of the silence, came a Presence that surrounded her. Was it an angel that came at times like this? That's what it felt like and she was always reluctant to move or look around for fear of disturbing the moment of sheer unearthly calm. She lived for these moments alone with her Heavenly Father—whatever form He was in.

Occasionally, she was able to have private conversation with her young brother-in-law, Donny. He was always ready to hear about her experiences with God—or read what He had given her to write down.

A scribe. That's what Pastor Judd Luke had called her. He showed her in the Bible where some were given the calling of a scribe—to write prophetically—Words that God speaks to them to record on paper.

It was an awesome, yet humbling calling, but at times, lonely. Most couldn't wrap their minds around such a thing—and didn't really *want* to know about it.

But Laura found that she couldn't get enough. She wanted more and more of Him as time went on. What she didn't know was what God wanted of her? What was she supposed to do with her life now?—Her time? These experiences with the Lord were so personal. Just between Him and her. Shouldn't this be helping someone else somewhere along the line? Even her own husband didn't want to hear about what was happening to her.

She knew Jesse was a strong believer in Jesus Christ. Jesus was his Lord. He prayed about everything. And it showed up in the love he had for her and their children—People, in general. He was more of a *giver* than she was. The shirt would come off his back without a single thought if he saw someone without one—or his boots, for that matter. She had seen him take off his boots and give them to a barefoot, homeless man in Jackson a couple years ago.

But for all that, he couldn't reckon with the idea of the God of the Universe speaking to her or anyone else in the manner that she was hearing Him.

Her heart suddenly felt heavy and unsure—of everything. She bent over with her face in her hands.

Lord God, help me understand what You want out of me. Is something wrong with me? Is it Your Voice I'm hearing? Am I being deceived some way? Help me, Lord.

Immediately she regained a peace—a calmness inside and she sat up. A Word, like in a vision, appeared in front of her—commanding her. **WRITE**

She switched the lamp on beside her chair and opened her notebook—pen in hand, and waited.

Words began to pour into her mind and she wrote—

Thus saith He whom loves you so—Daughter, My sheep hear My Voice. I AM the Light of the world. He who comes to Me, I will not cast aside. When you seek Me with your whole being, you will find Me. This you have done, My Laura. Fear not. Step out into the deeper waters, I called to you, and you did. Fear not. Follow Me.

She lay her notebook and pen aside and began to praise her Lord Jesus with words of love and thankfulness.

Donny had never been afraid of long hours of hard work. He'd felt like he'd been rode hard and put up wet, as the saying goes, many times. But tonight, after getting Jesse and Laura back home from the hospital and catching up on all the ranch chores that he, Jesse and Andy usually split—he had to literally pray his way up the stairs to the loft bedroom.

He'd heard that Beau Doss and Miss Jones were found and he met her brother, Dawson, just before Andy and the girl left for Jackson hospital to be with Beau.

The reunion between Dawson Jones and his young sister was a great ending to a harrowing day. Big brother had held her in a tight bear hug and cried until everybody in the Brandon kitchen teared up.

Dawson made the decision to catch the first flight possible back to California and drove the rental car to the airport right after his sister left for the hospital.

Then Donny headed out in the darkness and deep snow to feed and throw hay and break ice off the water tubs.

It was well after midnight when he dropped his coat, down vest and boots just inside the back door, stepped under a quick shower and headed upstairs in clean sweat pants and a tee shirt.

Reeny liked sleeping in the pitch-black dark, so he had to smile at the tiny night light plugged in to the wall at the top of the stairs. She had left it on for him and he figured it was a good thing she did. His head felt like it had a halo of fog around it and his legs wobbled with exhaustion.

At the top of the stairs, he pulled the night light out and dropped it on his bedside table and climbed into bed—literally. The bed was four thick mattresses high—a set-up Reeny saw in a magazine. She had a step-stool on her side. Usually he just took one good flying leap and he was in. Tonight—he climbed.

Moving with caution so he didn't disturb Reeny, who was lightly snoring, he eased his body onto the familiar God-send of a bed and...*OW*...*what the heck*... Something sharp jabbed him in the side and something else that felt like a book lumped beneath him.

He sat up and turned on the bedside lamp. There lay a pen and a spiral notebook in his spot! He scooped them up, noticing the notepad was open. A glance at it, as he was laying it beside his lamp, caused him to pause and look closer.

At the top of the page was written—Bonnie Brandon. Underneath her name was two columns—one titled, Boy and the other, Girl.

He scanned the names under each heading. They all began with the letter B, except one—Donny Jr., and it was written in larger letters than the others.

He raised his head up and stared at the wall in front of him. Bonnie would be almost six years old now. Starting school. But she had not been allowed to live even one moment on this earth. She was still-born under the most horrendous conditions possible—In a freezing cold cave, just out of reach of flood waters. She was Reeny's child from a rape, but the most perfectly formed little beauty. Donny proudly gave her his name.

He recalled the most awesome, purely supernatural event that allowed Reeny and him to escort her little soul into Heaven. Never, for all eternity, would he forget one detail of that near death experience. (This event is detailed in Surrendered IV)

Reeny had almost lost her life as well, but the doctors told the couple shortly after that traumatic event that Reeny had a slim to none chance of conceiving another child.

He glanced back down at the list of names. It was the Donny, Jr that did it. *Was...was she...?* He turned his head to stare at his sleeping bride of five years. He had to know. Right now.

He clicked off the lamp, lay down and rolled over until he had Reeny scooped into his spoon in the middle of their king sized bed.

She reached a hand behind her head and patted his cheek. "You finally made it home," she whispered.

"Yeah," he whispered back. "You left some notes—names written in your tablet. Was kinda wondering who—Donny Jr is?"

The emotion Reeny heard in his voice made her smile. She turned partly onto her back and reached for his hand, placing it on her thin, flat stomach. "He's right here."

The lump that he'd managed to ignore, instantly grew bigger until it made his eyes water. He raised up over her, only able to see the outline of her head. His large hands cradled her face.

"Are you... positive?"

"One hundred and ten percent. You're going to be a daddy." She could feel the trembling in Donny's chest where he was pressed against her.

"Oh, God," he choked against her ear. "Thank you, Jesus. Thank you, Reeny." He had sought God many times in the night with tears that He would allow Reeny to conceive a baby again. He thought if life got any better for him, he'd die of pure joy.

It was another hour before he managed to calm his weary bones and sleep.

Carly went in to sit with Beau. It was 5am and he still hadn't shown any improvement—still unconscious.

Web punched in Charlotte Doss's cell number. She answered on the second ring.

"Charlotte, Web Vance. I found Riley. He's in Wyoming." He told her the story—a short version. "He's in the hospital in Jackson. I'm with him now."

"Will he be alright?"

"He's still unconscious from a hard blow to the head."

"Well, I'll expect you to keep me posted. I can't leave here. I'm in the middle of a huge court case. Leo and I are both working night and day on this thing."

After disconnecting from the call, he had already decided to let Mrs. Doss call for information about her son—when she had time.

He would be here *until*.

He sucked a deep, steady breath and forced the woman's words out of his mind. He needed to be all here for *his* son and only death itself was going to be allowed to interfere. *That* he couldn't control.

Andy was stretched out on one of the couches in the waiting room. Web sat in a chair next to him.

The image of the young cowboy—boots with spurs still strapped on and a felt Stetson using his face for a hat rack—stirred Web's long past memory bank into a fresh, soul-stirring moment.

For a few seconds, he longed for those youthful days of the rodeo circuit—Miles and miles of hauling across one state line after another. Sometimes there was a stall for his horse—most times he tied him to the trailer while he slept on the seat of his 1972 single cab Custom Deluxe Chevy truck. He had to smile at the memory of that old banger, although it was a good one in it's day.

He had no responsibilities other than himself and his beloved Rascal. The dapple-grey gelding rode every mile he did and performed with expertise and a full heart that never waned. In Web's book, there would never be another horse born that could top him. Rascal was retired at the age of 25 and buried four years later on one of his roping buddy's family ranch in Arizona.

He'd gotten the call one morning early that old Rascal had died of natural causes out in knee-high prairie grass. He knew that would happen one day and swallowed the instant lump that had jumped to his throat. He flew out to see him buried. When he looked at him for the last time, grief dropped him to his knees and he'd cried until his tears had washed his great friend's face.

Web swiped at his eyes. That longing for those days quickly melted away as an unnatural and hated exhaustion from his illness suddenly squeezed the strength from his shoulders, arms and legs.

He rested his head on the back of his chair and wondered how young Andy knew who he was. His rodeo career had ended decades ago.

***

CHAPTER THIRTEEN

Beau could hear a constant beeping noise off in the distance. It was grating on his last nerve. He needed it to stop.

It seemed like he had to fight to get his eyes to open.

Finally, he climbed out of the darkness and the beeping became louder. He opened his eyes. His head hurt.

The light in the room was dim, but he could see the girl curled up in a chair beside his bed. He knew her—from somewhere, but he couldn't come up with a name.

There was a needle and tubes in his left hand. He was in a hospital. Slowly he accessed his situation and decided he must have been in an accident.

Carly jerked awake suddenly. She looked at Beau's face and found him staring at her.

She jumped to her feet. "You're awake! Oh, thank God."

"Where am I?" His voice was weak.

"Jackson Hospital." She was careful, not sure how much to tell him at this point.

"Why? What…happened to me?" His forehead crinkled in confusion.

"You took a hard hit to the side of your head."

"Who hit me?"

He clearly hadn't regained his memory. "You...um...were fighting a bad guy!" She gave him a half-hearted smile.

Before he could ask more questions, she asked him, "Do you know who I am?"

His squinted eyes searched her face and she already knew the answer.

"I'm...not sure. Should I?"

"I'm Carly Jones. We met at High Point Dude Ranch. You live in a small log cabin and I was staying in an Indian teepee."

"Wait. Wait a minute." He rubbed his free hand across his eyes. "Now—what!?" He tried to chuckle at the absurdity of what she'd said.

"Ohhh." He moaned and held his stomach. "Sick. I'm going to be sick." He raised up slightly and turned on his side.

She grabbed a spit cup off the table beside her and held it under his mouth while pressing the call button.

At that moment, a nurse and a doctor filed into the room and took charge.

"Take some deep breaths, Mr. Doss," the nurse instructed as she took the cup. "It'll help stop the nausea."

He did and finally lay back with the most intense headache he'd ever had.

The doctor examined the swelling on his head. "Nice to see you awake, Riley. Are you having a little pain?"

"A lot."

"A lot of pain. I'll get you something right now to help that." He gave the order for a hypo and the nurse wheeled and left.

"Can you tell me your whole name, son?"

"Riley Doss."

"Got a middle name?"

"Beau...Doss." He said it like he wasn't sure.

Quietly, Carly moved to stand at the foot of the bed where Beau could see her. Her heart leaped at the way he'd said, *Beau...Doss.* He seemed unsure of how to say his name.

He stared at her for a long moment, glanced at the doctor, then back at her. "Are you all right, Carly?"

Her heartbeat picked up speed. "Yes, I am. Do you remember what happened...Beau?"

"I don't know how I got here, but we were lost in the storm—Found a shelter to get in."

Oh, thank you, God. "Yes."

The nurse came in then and administered the shot. Within a minute, his countenance softened and relaxed as the pain left. He closed his eyes and drifted off.

"He'll sleep for a while now." The doctor nodded at Carly.

More than anything, she wished she could curl up beside him—hold him until he woke up.

"Will he be all right?"

"He's improving, hon. That's good news for now." The doc patted her shoulder as he walked around her and went out.

When she got back to the waiting area, the doc had just left after delivering the news to Web and Andy. She walked in-between them where they had stood to hear the report and put her arms around their waists. A group hug was called for.

Andy headed back to the ranch a few minutes later, after Carly and Web each found a spot to catch a nap.

For the first time ever, during the busy spring dude ranch activity time—there was quiet. Reservations were suspended for at least six weeks while Jesse's leg healed and Beau Doss's head injury had time to heal fully.

Hank and Martha kept the kitchen duty in full swing for the family, while Laura, Andy and Donny took care of other ranch chores, including caring for Beau throughout the day and night.

He'd been out of the hospital for a week, but required a lot of rest and scheduled meds. Andy took over most of Beau's care.

He wasn't able to recall everything that had happened to him and Carly—he remembered nothing about the man who had threatened their lives or that they had exchanged blows.

The snow had melted and spring was quickly making a comeback. Beau was feeling like his old self, but getting past Warden Granny Martha in order to get back to work had no chance whatsoever. The woman was a tall, skinny pain in his rear, but he loved her as if she was his own granny.

He still had a week or so before the doctor would release him to ride. The Brandon's had insisted he stay in his cabin and let them help him recover, but demanded he wait for a medical release before doing any ranch work. He agreed, but fully intended to make up for this beautiful family's time and money spent on him.

All of those things he knew he could eventually deal with. He did *not* know how he was going to handle the gut-twisting hurt that Carly Jones had left him with. There wasn't a medicine to help that pain.

He thought they'd had more going between them than what she evidently did—leaving for California without so much as a *get well soon.*

The sun was almost down on another day. Beau kicked his recliner all the way back and stretched his cramped muscles, wishing he had one of those knock-out hypos he had in the hospital. The night would pass in a minute or less and he wouldn't lay in the dark feeling a beautiful, warm body snuggled against his—one that wasn't there.

Work. He needed to get back in the saddle and ride and get hot, sweaty and dirty, until he could do nothing else but fall exhausted into bed. Then get up and go again.

Just a few days, Beau, he encouraged himself. No one would know but him, so he let the pent-up tears slide down. *Why, God?*

Carly spent her first night back home sleeping in a lounge chair beside Webber Vance's hospital bed.

Beau was still too sick to be told who Web was and Web's illness had reached a point where he had no choice, but to return home to the cancer institute as soon as possible. He was hoping his doctors might help buy him a little more time.

Carly couldn't let him go alone. He was too weak to make it without help.

Beau had been semi-sedated, due to some tests he'd just received, when she went to tell him goodbye. He didn't understand that she would be coming back—only that she was leaving for California. In a half conscious state, he'd physically pushed her away and cursed at her. He was looking at her when he did it and appeared to know what he was doing. With a crushed heart and soul, she left.

"Carly?"

"Right here, Mr. Vance." She jumped up to stand by the bed.

Web reached out for her hand and wrapped it tight in his own.

She felt her heart swell and fill with sadness. Everything felt so wrong—what was happening to this man. He wanted so much to have the chance to know his son. And Beau to know him. *Dear God in Heaven, please give him more time.*

"Carly, I want you to go home now, honey. You don't need to be here with a crotchety old man. And anyway, I'm feeling better." He lifted his arm with the IV stuck in it. "They're packing me full of goodies. I'll be good for a while."

"But…"

"No! No *buts.*" He jostled her hand back and forth for emphasis. "Now, listen. You know where I hide the extra key to the building. Get it, go in and get what I left for you. It's in the file cabinet in my office. Top drawer. Do you remember the combination?"

"Yes."

"It's enough to tide you over until you find another job."

Oh! She hadn't thought about the fact that she was unemployed. Everything in her life seemed to have come to an end at once. Everything!

Her chin started to crinkle—emotion rushing at her from everywhere.

"No, now, don't do that or I'll start blubberin' and snotin' and you'll have to endure one of those 20/20 hindsight things. Don't…do…it!"

She laughed aloud then, fighting hard to keep the laughter from turning into sobs.

"Go see your family. They had a scare over all this."

She leaned down and kissed his forehead as he released her hand. "I will, but I'll be back to visit tomorrow."

He nodded and watched her disappear out the door, thankfully before his own chin jerked and tears rolled.

Carly ducked into the ladies room down the hall before she lost her fight. She locked the stall door and cried into her hands for Web, for life's injustices, for a father and son who never got to be—for Beau Doss. Her heart was in a million pieces. She needed to talk to her mom.

Web had rented a Ford Fusion at the airport for one month and told her to get his money's worth for him. As sick as he was, he took care of her needs. How did this beautiful person stay single—as far as she knew, his whole life.

When she got to the office, she opened the file cabinet and found an envelope with her name handwritten on the front. Inside was a sizable check made out to her along with a note stating that part of the money was for her P.I. Job and the rest was severance pay. The amount was staggering—enough to keep her going for many months. How would she ever be able to thank him, even if there was enough time?

A few minutes later, she exited onto the freeway, realizing she should let her mom know she was coming, but had no idea where her cell phone was. Probably down in one of her bags, with a dead battery, no doubt. She headed for her parents home, hoping her brothers were still there—feeling almost desperate to see their faces.

Andy rode out early, just before day break. The snow was melted, but a chill still hung in the morning air He had his own small herd of beef cattle on two hundred acres left to him by his dad. He didn't remember him, but his mom had only spoken good things about him.

He'd been killed in a car accident when Andy was four. Ironically, his father, Mathew Parker and his now, step-dad, Jesse Brandon, had been best friends—grew up as teens working for a Mr. Lex Farmer in Oklahoma somewhere.

Jesse had told him funny stories of his and his dad's escapades—each always trying to out-cowboy the other—both ending up with mud, blood and poop stuck in their ears and elsewhere.

He smiled at those memories now, knowing someday he'd get to tell those stories, as well as his own, to his kids.

Beau Doss had been his sidekick since he'd brought him to High Point. He missed the camaraderie—wondered if that was how his dad and Jesse were in their younger years. He understood it because he and Beau had become like brothers the past year.

Just then, his mare's ears perked and her head shot up on high alert. He pulled her to a sudden stop and sat erect. There was a lone horse and rider about three hundred yards ahead, the rider staring him down like a rattler about to strike. Then the two horses whinnied a greeting and the rider stuck his hand up.

Beau! Andy trotted over to him. "Man, you aren't supposed to be on a horse yet. How long you been doing this?"

Beau grinned. "Couple days."

Andy shook his head. "Dad knows you were doing this without a doctor's release, and I knew about it, he'd send me out to break him off a switch."

Beau threw back his head and laughed hard and loud. "Think I'll tell him just so I can watch that." He laughed more.

"Well, might as well make the rounds with me."

They fell in side by side at a slow walk.

"Sure feels good to be in this saddle. I never would have guessed that my life would have gone in this direction."

"Yeah, your story is a strange one all right. But that's God's way. Pastor Judd said that He can take the most unlikely candidate for a job and equip him to go do it."

Beau nodded. "Don't suppose they know anything yet about the dead man or who lived in that dug-out?"

"As a matter of fact, the sheriff was out last night. I was going to fill you in today. The autopsy showed the man died of a massive heart attack."

Beau let out the breath he was holding. "Thank God! After Carly said I had cold cocked him with a chunk of wood, I was afraid I had…" His voice broke.

"Nope, you didn't take his life, but you can bet you'd still be a hero if you had."

"No. No. I obviously wasn't even conscious. Spare me the hero thing."

"You saved Carly's life and yours, to hear her tell it. And everything appears to add up to the story you both told."

"Who was he?"

"Escaped convict from a prison in Texas. Sheriff said he'd been hiding for fifteen years. They ID'd him from fingerprints. He was in for life—for murdering an elderly couple and stealing their car."

"Wow. Wonder how long he lived in that hole in the ground?"

"Don't know, but I think the investigation is over with. They bagged up everything and cleaned it out."

Both men were silent for a while. They rode across acres of open grassland, the heifers with new babies making sure the interlopers knew they were being watched.

Andy counted six new calves on the ground, all bedded down close together in the breaking dawn. He felt like a proud papa. This was his first crop of babies. He couldn't wait to tell his dad and Hank.

Beau was sitting with one leg hiked up and resting across the cantle of his saddle. He appeared to be watching his buddy gush over his babies, but when Andy glanced over at him, he knew he was a long way off—California would be his guess.

Andy didn't know what prompted Carly and Webber to fly home so suddenly. He felt something was wrong, but these people were strangers and they had lives and jobs to get on with.

It still didn't make sense that Webber left without telling Beau who he was. It's not like he had abandoned him as a baby or anything.. The man didn't know he had a son. Except—now he knows—and he just up and left. And Carly Jones, too.

His mind was racing with the story Carly told him—urging him to tell all he knew to his friend. He'd told his mom, dad and Hank the story to stop their worries about Web's strange attention to Beau.

But then, he recognized that quiet urging deeper down inside of him to **Be Still.** A picture formed in his mind when he heard those quiet, gentle Words and he knew he'd just received his answer from the Lord. He knew what he should do to help Beau and Web.

Andy could hardly think of anything else the rest of the day. He knew so well the power of prayer. He was beyond excited about what the Lord showed him early that morning.

Beau went back to his cabin and took the last of his meds. He fixed his own breakfast as he had for the past few days. He'd been helping with feed chores and mucking stalls— sneaking a quick ride before daylight. But riding out with Andy early this morning was what he needed to feel like his old self.

Hank had driven him in to Jackson for his doctor's appointment. He promptly delivered his final release to Jesse when they returned just before dark.

"Glad to see this, Beau. At least you'll be *legal* when you saddle up in the dark. Feel free to use the barn lights from now on."

"Yessir," was all he could manage. He grinned as he headed out to take care of the petting zoo animals. He felt like a kid being scolded by his dad. For some dumb reason, he suddenly had to swallow a huge lump in his throat, as he headed to his cabin.

Andy came in after dark from day-work at the Luke's place. He unsaddled and brushed his horse, fed and watered him as fast as he could.

He got to the back door of the house just as Gramps and Granny Walton were coming out to go home.

"Could you two wait a few minutes before you go. I need a family conference."

"You bet," Martha said. She cut her eyes at Hank and he shook his head to let her know he didn't have a clue what was going on.

They followed him inside, waiting until he boot-jacked his sock feet free, hung up his hat and coat.

"Mom!"

"In here, honey." Laura stood up from her rocker and layed the novel she was reading face down on the chair.

Jesse was lounging on the love seat with his leg propped up. He was in a walking cast now and getting around more than he should. He swung his leg down and sat up straight at the urgency in Andy's voice.

Everyone was staring at him as though he was about to deliver bad news. "Nothing's wrong. I've just been waiting all day for this. Is Uncle Donny and Aunt Reeny home?"

"No, they've gone out for the evening," Laura answered. "What's going on, Andy?"

"Early this morning, the Lord spoke to my spirit when I was thinking about telling Beau about Webber Vance being his real father. HE stopped me and said, *Be Still.* Then I saw an image in my mind of us—of my family here all gathered to pray for God to bring Beau together with his dad. God called this prayer meeting. HE's going to do something."

"Oh, Praise the Lord." Laura felt her spirit tremble in witness to Andy's words.

Hank immediately jerked his hat off of his head and tossed it behind him on a straight-backed chair.

Jesse stood and everyone began reaching for hands to form a circle.

"It is written," Andy began, *"where two or more are gathered together in MY NAME, there I AM in the midst of them. And it is written, Let your requests be made known unto ME. Lord, according to YOUR Word, we..."* emotion overwhelmed him then and Jesse took over.

"Lord, we plain and simply ask YOU to do what only YOU can do and bring this father and son together. We know, by YOU calling us to pray and ask in Beau and Webber's behalf, that this is YOUR perfect will for them. Thank YOU for what

YOU are going to do—In the Name of Jesus Christ." They all said *"Amen,"* in unison.

Andy covered his eyes with one hand, his shoulders shaking. Jesse hobbled over and put his arms around his man/son.

He knew Andy was reacting from his own life without his real dad, Matt Parker, as well as the desire he had for his friend to have his. Jesse just held him tight while everyone else reached for tissues and fought to dry their tears.

Hank and Martha went quietly out the back door. After Hank climbed behind the wheel of their pickup, he put his head onto the backs of his hands that gripped the steering wheel and cried like he had never cried for his own dad, for his mom and the injustices that seemed to weave through everyone's life that's ever lived on this earth.

Martha scooted across the seat and wrapped both arms around him, pressing her cheek against his back. It was a while before he raised up and put his arm around his wife—and kissed her with far more fervency and sweetness than he had in a very long time.

***

CHAPTER FOURTEEN

Juliette Doss was in Jackson Hole, Wyoming. It had taken the entire trip from California to get control over her rioting insides. Her mind was in turmoil in a way she had never experienced before, and she was at a loss to understand the intensity of how she felt.

Riley was her twin brother, but they were never particularly close. They never had developed the bond that twins usually did. She used to think it was because they were not the same sex. But now—

She'd had no preparation—no gentle easing up to the bombshell her mother had dropped on her just last week. She just let her rip, then dared to get her nose all out of joint because Juliette had responded with shock and tears.

Of all the freakish things in the world that could happen— and it happened to her and Riley. Twins—carried in their mother's belly and born three minutes apart, but fathered by two different men. Leonard Doss was her daddy, but not Riley's. Dear God!

Was that why he left the state and didn't tell a soul where he was going? Her mom had stopped at giving Julie a name or any information on the man—just told her that Riley now knew about him—that he was with his son and her brother at the hospital after he'd been injured out in a snow storm. She wished now that she had demanded more details from her mom, but something inside her exploded with a need to find him—To see for herself what was happening to him.

Riley was always quiet and with-drawn from everyone. He kept to himself and stayed home a lot. Mostly alone—while she always looked for friends to hang out with and spend nights with.

She never thought that much about her brother, until now. *Now,* she needed to find him—To see his face. He was her brother. Even if he didn't want or need her, she needed him. Strangely, she felt terribly lonesome for him.

It was dark and when she swung open the door of her Toyota Lexus in front of her motel, the cold air hitting her face surprised her. The clothes she brought would not be enough. She'd have to purchase a jacket tomorrow.

Right now, she was physically and emotionally drained. The Diamond Express had her bed and it was calling her name.

By 9AM, Julie was on the road to High Point Dude Ranch.

Of all the freekin' places on this earth, why was her brother in a God-forsaken place like this—if there was a God. And if there was a God, she'd never seen hide nor hair of Him.

She had heard people talk about their God—Jesus—or whatever they called Him, like He was a real thing. Like they personally knew Him. What a crock!

Julie had relied on no one but herself, her entire life. She came and went when she was a kid without any restrictions. No rules. She always had girls ready to buddy with her, mainly because she always had money to spend and gave them her high-priced clothes and shoes.

She'd always been a little on the heavy side—not the cheerleader type the boys went for, but her mom made sure she was well supplied to buy her way through that problem.

After high school, she entered law school because her parents were both lawyers and rich and she wanted to continue to live with money to burn. And—because Leonard and Charlotte Doss loved her for walking in their footsteps. That was new and she desperately wanted to hold on to her parent's attention and approval. They loved her more than they loved Riley. That wasn't fair, but maybe he should have stayed in school and made something of himself—become somebody they could be proud of.

Even as these same old justifications rolled through her head, she knew deep inside that something was very wrong—with her.

Riley's life may be off in the armpit of the country, but she was living a lie in the lap of luxury. And neither one felt right—Riley's nor hers.

What was happening to her? Why did her whole life seem to be upside down just because she found out Riley had a different daddy?

Life was going the way she'd planned it for herself. She was a successful lawyer in her parent's law firm. She knew and partied with all the higher-ups in town—and out of town.

So, whatever issues she thought she might be having, really had to do with her rebellious brother. She just needed to show him what real success looked and lived like now that they were adults.

Oh, God, she felt like she was losing her mind—Thoughts running amuck with no solid bottom in them. Confusion reigned.

She pulled her car onto the narrow shoulder and stopped. Tears cascaded down her face in uncontrollable sheets. "Why…Mom? She sobbed into her hands.

It was an idyllic morning—a cool, crispy spring day to look forward to. The whole crew was mounted and ready for a long day of ranch chores and day-work.

Beau glanced at each cowboy—all family members—and listened to their bantering back and forth. There wasn't a curse word in any of the mouthy and joking comments. Just good natured bantering.

Donny Brandon, Andy, Grandpa Hank and even Jesse was in the saddle, his walking cast hanging like a led weight.

Beau chuckled to himself. He couldn't keep the thankful grin from pulling at his mouth, his head shaking in pure awe of Almighty God's goodness to him. Only God could have picked him up out of the lonely, loveless solitude he'd lived all his life and dropped him into this Heavenly bliss. Who knew he could take on this lifestyle so easily—but Him?

"We're burning daylight, *dudes,*" Jesse bellowed. "It'll be lunch time before we get out of the yard. Head em' up."

A second later, all heads turned at the sound of a vehicle coming into the yard. The fancy bright red Lexus commanded attention—the California license tags not lost on any of them.

Beau's mouth dropped open. He knew the car and that was plain to all the rest.

Julie wondered if she had driven up on an old western movie set—cowboys and horses all ready to go. *Is this for real?*

Jesse motioned at Donny to greet the visitor. He was a little hard pressed to get off and on his horse.

He quickly dismounted and walked to the driver's open window, leading his horse. "Good morning, mam. Donny Brandon." He offered his hand in the window.

"Hi. I'm Juliette Doss. I'm looking for my brother, Riley."

Donny wasn't familiar with the name Riley, but he turned and saw Beau step off his horse and come toward the car.

"Beau, this is…"

He put up a hand and nodded at Donny to stop the introductions. "Go ahead Donny. I'll catch up."

"Pleasure to meet you, Juliette." He nodded his head toward her, mounted up and rode back to the others. He swung his arm toward the gate behind the barn. "Let's go."

Beau had stopped a few feet from her car and stood waiting for her to get out. She hadn't changed in the year since he'd seen her, but it was obvious she had no clue who he was. His hair was long, curled around the back of his neck and his short growth of black stubble and straw Stetson shading his face— not to mention the horse he was leading—Did not add up to Riley Doss.

She got out and before he let her embarrass herself with an introduction, he said, "Hey, Julie." He grinned and she sucked her breath in with a gasp.

"Riley?"

Even when she said his name, he could tell she wasn't fully convinced it was him. This *man* was taller and muscled and better looking than her brother. And he rode a horse? But the voice was Riley's and his grin was Riley.

"Riley?"

He couldn't hold in the chuckle. "It's me—Riley Beaumont Doss, a.k.a your twin brother."

She stared at him, her brown eyes widening.

He held the geldings reins loosely behind him, walked up and put his free arm around her shoulders for a quick hug. When he stepped back, her eyes fell to his boots and the spurs that jangled every time he took a step. The shocked gaze travelled slowly back up to his grinning face. She couldn't decide if she liked what she saw or not.

"How…I mean…how did all this happen?"

"Well, we'll have to sit down and talk about that later. Long story. How did you find me?"

"Mom."

Confusion creased his face. "Mom…what? Is she and Dad alright?"

"They're fine. Mom told me where you were. I just…felt like I needed to check on you. You disappeared, Riley, without a word."

He nodded. "Yes. I had nothing better to do. It's been a year, Julie. When did anyone miss me and how did Mom know where I was?"

She looked hard at him. His voice was edged with anger, but this bantering back and forth was confusing.

They both turned their heads toward the slam of the ranch house back door.

"Beau! Hey, Beau!" Jesse, Jr. was running toward them, grinning from ear to ear—always happy about something.

"Hey, little buddy." Beau grabbed him up and hugged him tight before setting him back on his feet.

"Beau, are you staying here today? I could help you work."

Beau? Julie eyed her brother and then the little boy like she was seeing something she didn't believe.

He squatted down to Jesse Jr.'s size. "Tell you what, Little Jess. I'll come get you this evening and you can help me feed the zoo. Right now, I've got…"

-336 "There you are." Laura walked up and took her son's hand. "Sorry, Beau."

"Not a problem. Laura, this is my sister, Julie."

"Julie. I'm Laura Brandon." She reached out and shook hands. "I'm so happy to meet you and welcome to High Point. I'm headed to town, but hopefully we'll meet again while you're here."

The genuiness of Laura's smile caused a tremble in Julie's insides. Her smile was not just with her mouth, but her eyes. The difference was astounding. "Thank you, Mrs. Brandon." Something made her want to follow her, to talk to her about—anything.

Beau pointed to the barn and told her to park there while he put his horse up. They definitely had some visiting to do!

She watched him step up on the big reddish colored horse and ride off like a—real cowboy. Was she just asleep and dreaming all this?

"Carly Anne Jones, whatever gets into you, I'll never know. You sure don't take after your mother!"

"Dad, I'm fine." She had just spent the past hour detailing her adventure in Wyoming to her parents. Her brothers had already left for their own homes. "What was it you used to say—*All's well that ends well.* Well!" She slapped her hands on her hips and dared him to deny his own old saying.

"That could have ended a lot different if…"

"All right, you two. Supper is ready. And she is not me or you, big guy. She's Carly. She's home and she's safe. Now lets eat."

Lindsey Jones was a *take it how it comes and keep it real* kind of mom, but Carly didn't miss the fear that she saw drop over her as she related the details of her and Beau Doss's experience in the Wyoming snow storm.

And Mom, being mom to her only daughter, didn't miss the pain that had slipped into her story every time she mentioned the name Beau. She knew Carly was old enough to experience her life, her way—but she could sense her daughter needing to say more than what she'd told them of her adventure.

"Well, all the same, I plan on having a few words with this boss of yours. What's his name again?"

"Ex-boss, Dad. He…"

"So, he nearly gets you killed and then fires you! For what!?"

She rolled her eyes, but only in an attempt to stave off the tears that were suddenly burning them. It didn't work and she stood up from the dining table. "Excuse me," she whispered, and hurried up the stairs to her old room.

Laying in the middle of her bed, curled into a fetal position and sobbing was how Lindsey found her. Her heart broke at the sight. Something horrific had happened to her little girl. She sat down on the edge of the bed and leaned over her daughter. With her arms cradling her, she put her face close to Carly's as though to absorb some of her pain.

After a minute, Carly pushed upward and her mom sat up and released her.

"I'll be okay, Mom."

"I know you will, honey. After all, you're *my* daughter. Would you like to talk about things? I'm all yours."

She rubbed her face with both hands. "No. Yes. Oh God, Mom, Mr. Vance is dying. He has pancreatic cancer and Beau Doss is his son, but Beau doesn't know he's his son."

Lindsey sucked a deep breath. "I'm not getting the fullness of all this, but enough to know you have a right to be overwhelmed. Let's back up and slow down a little."

She related the story that Webber had told her in the hospital waiting room.

"And I *had* to help Mr. Vance get home. He's so sick. And Beau doesn't know he's his father."

"Mercy, Carly. That's a lot for a young woman to deal with."

"It's not either of their fault. Neither one knew about the other. Except her. Beau's mother knew from the time he was fourteen. And now Webber is going to die soon."

Both were quiet for a while. Lindsey watched her daughter gaze off into space, a lonely, lost expression coating her face that Lindsey could read too well.

"Is it Beau?"

She slowly turned her face to her mom. "What?"

"The one you're missing so terribly. Is it Beau Doss?"

Stunned, her eyes widened on her mother.

Lindsey simply nodded. "How serious did you and he become?"

After a long silence, "I love him, Mom. I can't stand being away from him."

"Does he know this?"

"I don't know. So much happened in the middle of…"

"Falling in love?" she finished for her. "Do you believe he loves you, too."

"I…I thought he did."

Slowly, Lindsey bobbed her head up and down. She refused to remember—even quietly to herself—the details of her first love. It was so long ago, but now, after all the years of marriage and children, there was still a small space in her heart that was never filled. It held the pain of longing for many years, for a love that anger and foolish pride had caused her to turn her back on. And even now, when she forced herself to look inside, the space was still there and still empty.

"Then you have to go back and find out."

Carly shot an incredulous look at her mom. "But, I…don't know how to do that."

It'll come naturally if you and this young man are truly in love. If you discover there isn't anything between you now, come home. You've lost nothing. But if there is…."

Before she could finish, Carly threw her arms around her beautiful, understanding mother and squeezed her hard.

Lindsey laughed and hugged her back.

"I have to go see Web tomorrow. Oh, God, please let him be better. Let him be strong enough to make the trip with me. Please God! Amen."

Lindsey found her daughter's hasty little prayer touching, even though she would not have thought about praying. She believed God was real, but figured whatever happened to people was each one's own doing. Everybody just got what they got in life.

"Mom, do me a favor. After I'm gone, tell Dad my ex-boss's name is Web Vance and show him the calf roper's picture hanging over the TV." She winked at her mom's questioning stare. "It'll calm him down."

Beau walked Julie on a tour around the ranch, giving her a clear picture of where he lived now. He explained his work and told her about his day-work on the Double OO Ranch a few miles up the road.

He would catch that, *I'm not believing this,* look now and again and each time he felt himself stand a little taller and prouder of himself. He'd never realized what all he *had* accomplished since coming here until he listened to himself telling it to his sister.

"You actually *rope* cows from a *horse?*"

His laughter was genuinely joyful and she couldn't keep from smiling at that while shaking her head in disbelief.

"Yes. I guess I sort of have a natural knack for it. That's what they tell me, anyway. Here's where I live." He stopped a few steps from his cabin and let her look.

"No way, Riley. You like living in that…that Daniel Boone cabin? Seriously?"

"Well, it was either this or one of the Indian teepees. They're not half bad, but I like the privacy of this place. It's sort of back here by itself."

He went inside ahead of her, waiting while she reluctantly stepped through the doorway. He left the door open.

"Can I get you something to drink? There's no soda, but coffee or tea?"

"No, thanks."

"Have a seat. We need to talk."

She sat stiffly on the edge of the leather loveseat, even though she was surprised at how clean the place was.

"You go first," he offered. "What do you want to know?"

"How did you get here?"

"Well, once upon a time, I was sitting in a bus station, minding my own business..."

Julie remained spell-bound as she listened to him recall every step he had taken from that bus station until today, including all he could recall of his and Carly's snow storm adventure."

"But, the short version is—Almighty God took pity on me and brought me to Heaven—early. And if you *know* that I'm just asleep and dreaming all this, don't make the mistake of waking me up. Better let this sleeping dog alone."

She laughed aloud and finally relaxed. She didn't know if she wanted to try and save her idiot twin from this going-no-where existence or be jealous of him. "Well, I guess that leads me to my next question.?" Whether he realized it or not, she caught the drain in his expression, a sadness, every time he mentioned that girl's name. "What's the deal with you and this Carly Jones?"

The look he shot her then, told her all but the fine details.

"I believe it's my turn."

"Ah. Sorry, go for it." She could hardly wait for her turn again.

"How did Mom know where I was?"

"You should already know that. Your father called her when you were in the hospital. He was up here with you."

He gazed off into space, squinting his eyes, trying to remember. Most of his hospital stay was a little hazy.

He looked back at her. "Dad was up here?"

Her eyes squinted then. "No. Not *Dad. Your* …um…father. Your real father…sperm donor…whatever you call him."

Beau ran his hand across his chin, not taking his eyes off of her. His grin was a lopsided smirk. "*My* dad was here—but not *your* dad."

Then it hit him. "Oh, I get it. What did you and Dad do— finally have a big blow-up?"

Stricken, she covered her mouth with her hand and shook her head. "No, Riley…you *don't* get it. You don't know. Oh God—she said you knew! Mom said you knew!"

"Knew what, Juliette? You aren't making sense."

"You better get a real tight grip on yourself. This is not going to be easy to hear."

"I'm a big boy. Spill it."

After a very long pause and a deep breath—"It's rare, but twins can be fathered by two different men if the conditions are just right."

"What…conditions?"

"Riley...Mom had another boyfriend for a short time before she got with Dad and married him. She obviously went from one bed right to the other and—we were conceived at that time. My father is Leonard Doss. Your's...is someone else."

He slouched back into his seat and stared blankly at nothing out in front of him.

The silence in that little cabin was deafening. It was hard to breathe normally, but Julie didn't speak or move a muscle. She knew he was trying to process what he'd just heard. She didn't care how much time he needed. She'd wait.

Finally, after a very long silence—"How long has she known this?"

"Since you tested to give me a kidney when we were fourteen."

"Does Da...Leonard Doss know I'm not his?"

"Yes."

His head moved slowly, up and down. *"That* ...explains it...why I was left to myself like an orphan. Neither of them acted like they knew I was alive."

"Riley, you know very well I was treated the same way that you were."

"Why, Julie? Why were we not wanted?"

"It wasn't us. It was them. They were just too busy climbing the old proverbial ladder of success—being *somebody.*"

"And if their kids both became lawyers, *they* would look even better. Hotshot parents."

"Something like that."

The taste of bile rose in Julie's throat, bitter and vile. She was no better than they were. That self-absorbed blood was running thick and nasty in her veins—full blood and it showed. For the first time, she saw the lifestyle of the rich for what it was when there was no deposit of heart or soul to go with it.

Riley's gaze was at nothing out in front of him, but he felt quietly peaceful. "Have you ever wondered how on earth those two found each other. They're just alike—dead to everything that is not about them."

She raised her eyebrows. "No, I've never thought of that. But I have searched for some good memories of our growing-up years." She looked at him, "I didn't find any."

Just then her mind brought up a picture of Laura Brandon's smile. The twinkling smile—the acceptance she saw in her eyes. A longing crushed through her heart that made her eyes sting.

Then she remembered something else—The time when she was thirteen and sitting in a restaurant with her parents. Their waitress was a middle-aged woman with short greying hair and no make-up. The lady came to take their orders and when Julie couldn't decide what to eat, the woman placed an arm around her shoulders and bent down close to her, pointing out what was good on the menu and smiling at her as though she was someone special. Like a mother might do.

She couldn't remember what she had finally ordered, but the loving touch and acceptance of that woman remained her favorite childhood memory—to this day. She seemed to function off of that one touch from then on.

"You know, Julie, our lives could have been a lot different."

She turned a hard, even gaze on him.

He met it with a slight smile. "A *bad* kind of different. We weren't abused physically or left hungry and without *things.* So…we raised ourselves, but in the lap of luxury. And here we are, twenty-four years old, you have a law degree and a great job. I found a life that I love more than anything money could buy me. The people here…my friends…it's like living and working in Heaven."

He paused thoughtful, "You know what I truly believe?"

She slowly shook her head, astounded at the words coming out of his mouth.

"I believe God has given me back all the good parts that was denied me while I was a kid—love, friends, acceptance for who I am. Happiness. Everything. There's nothing I need or…"

He stopped short and after a moment she finished for him, "Want?"

He didn't respond.

"I *knew* it, Riley Doss…or…whoever you are."

"Sorry," she muttered, when he cocked a glare her way. "But you have a real thing for that girl…Carly Jones. It's all over you."

Beau was shocked at that, but immediately slapped his hands down on both knees and stood. "Julie, I've got to get to work. You're welcome to stay here. There's food in the kitchen. I'm sure it's okay if you want to ramble around the grounds. I'll be back in by dark."

She simply nodded as he popped his hat on and hurried out.

How did she know? All he'd said about Carly was the fact they'd gotten lost in the storm and found shelter.

Memories came then of her curled up in his arms as he kept her warm—He couldn't go past that. The tightness in his throat was threatening to choke off his air.

Julie had walked toward the barn in time to watch her little brother, younger by three minutes, head off across the pasture like he was part of the horse he rode—handsome, confident and broken hearted.

But, she knew Riley had found a place for himself—a good life and hopefully, in time, someone to share it with.

Julie returned to his cabin, wrote a quick goodbye note and left for home. Just maybe that God he spoke about would help her find a good life for herself, too.

***

CHAPTER FIFTEEN

Beau loped toward the far end of the ranch where a new fence was being strung. He needed to take his place unrolling barbed wire, but for the first time since coming here, his heart wasn't in it.

Spurring his horse, he turned and headed to the opposite side where the little cabin called Honeymoon Hideout set. He had no idea why he headed there, other than to be somewhere totally private. There were no guests on the ranch this week and he knew where all the hands were working.

The hitching post on the side of the cabin was rotten and about to pull out of the ground. He made a mental note to come later and put in a new one. He tied up to a tree limb and went inside.

He'd already toured the cabin with Andy so he knew there was coffee and all the stuff to go with it in the kitchen.

While the coffee brewed, he sat on the bench at the small log dining table. Right off, he realized this was good for too much time to think, which he didn't need.

The question burned in his mind until it burned hot tears in his eyes. *Who am I? Who is my father? What is my name?*

The emotion he felt wasn't because he was not a Doss. The story his twin sister just told him should have rocked his world off its axis. Strangely, that didn't happen. Maybe it would hit him broadside later. But he doubted it. He felt disconnected, but only because he didn't know his own name.

Leonard Doss was no loss to him. He'd made it plain everyday of Beau's life that he didn't care if he lived or died. He'd never formed any kind of a bond with the man that he'd believed was his father. There was no close connection to his mother either. Neither of them wanted to be parents to Julie and him.

He felt a strange sense of freedom. And the strong aroma of coffee that filled the little secluded log cabin in the woods somehow just soothed his soul.

He moved to the small red leather sofa that faced the cleaned-out fireplace and sipped his hot drink. It was in that instance that he remembered something—Two things of real significance.

One, Jesse Brandon had told him that his hospital bill was anonymously paid in full.

And two, his sister had said that his *father* had been with him at the hospital.

He also had been told, through the haze of his head injury, that it was Carly Jones's boss who had come from California to join the search and he was the one who found them. He didn't recall meeting him in the hospital, but then his memory of most of that time was bits and pieces. *That* would be way too much of a coincidence anyway. Carly would have known and she'd have told him.

Carly. His throat tightened.

Andy had seen Beau coming toward them a few hours ago and had an idea where he may have gone when he suddenly switched direction. Whatever his sister had come here for must have upset him. Never had he shirked his work. In fact, Beau always went over and beyond what was asked of him.

For the past half hour, Jesse sensed his son's unrest. His mind was not on his wire stretching. He had seen Beau ride past, too.

"Son, go on and check on him. We're about done here."

Andy's eye went to his dad's leg cast, but a quick jerk of Jesse's head in the direction Beau went told him he wasn't the only one concerned.

Andy mounted up and rode straight for the Honeymoon cabin. Jake was tied to a limb and standing relaxed. He noticed the falling hitching post as he rode by.

He dismounted and dropped his reins—Sugar Beet was well trained to ground tie.

He knocked once.

"It's open."

Andy opened the door and stuck his head in. "Want company? Yes or no."

"Yeah." He raised his arm and motioned with his fingers, then slapped the seat cushion beside him.

"Thought you might be out here." Andy sat and neither spoke for a while. The silence was comfortable. The two men had formed a bond, beginning the evening Beau had agreed to go home to High Point with him. He remembered out loud Andy's first words when he'd walked up to him in the Burger Gettin' Place. "*So you're the one.*"

What?"

"That's the first thing you said to me the night I got to town. Not—Hello, I'm Andy. Just, *So you're the one.* He bugged out his eyes. "What was that about?"

Andy laughed. "Took you long enough to ask. Truth is, God told me to go to that place at that time. He didn't say what I was going there for, but when I saw you, I knew inside, by the Holy Spirit, you were the reason I was sent there. I just did what came to mind and now—here we sit. A year later and *you,* who'd never ridden a horse in his life, is out-riding, out-roping and out-girlfriending *me.* I should have left your butt there with your burger and fries."

Beau felt his chest suddenly swell with emotion. "My name's not Doss."

Andy heard the crack in his voice, clamped his mouth shut and looked at his friend.

"It's not?" Andy decided he'd better be nonchalantly dumb until he figured out what was going on.

"My name is Riley Beaumont—somebody. I don't know who the *somebody* is."

Andy looked at the floor. He was stunned that Beau didn't know. "You have a sister—a twin. Did she just find this out?"

"Yeah. But that's just the thing. We're twins, born three minutes apart. But…her name *is* Doss. I have a different father. Did you know that was possible?"

Disbelief coated Andy's face. "No. When…when did you learn this?"

"This morning. Juliette."

Andy suddenly felt like he was being squeezed in a vise. He knew part of this. He'd learned it from Carly. And he knows who Beau's father is—Never suspecting Beau didn't know. But—twins with two different dads?

He created himself a minute to think. "So…how long will your sister be here?"

He shook his head. "Don't know. She didn't come here just to tell me *that,* because she thought I already knew. Mom told her my *father* was at the hospital with me." His head jerked up like the whole thing just hit him. "Somebody paid my bill. Andy, you were there and Carly, too, most of the time—at the hospital, I mean."

Here it comes. Lord God, help me out here. How am I supposed to handle this?

Andy was quiet as he stared at the floor and Beau stared at him.

"You know something about this. What are you not telling me?" He waited, sensing he was about to get an answer that he just hoped he was ready for.

After a long couple minutes, "Do you know *anything* about professional rodeo?"

Beau cut a frustrated frown over at him and slowly shook his head.

"Well, I do. Especially the pro-ropers that follow the circuit. I've met several of them and then there's older ones that I've just read about—like this older cowboy who used to rope a lot when he was younger. A whole lot."

"Andy—this better be worth my time to listen to because I'm not much in the mood for..."

Without looking up, Andy continued, "In fact, he was a world champion roper, not once, but five times. That's big stuff in rodeo. He's a legend."

Beau still had his eyes slanted at him. "So?" He was really needing Andy to knock it off.

"So...well...he was the one who paid your hospital bill."

Beau raised his head and slowly turned fully around to face Andy. His eyes grew as he processed what he was just told.

"Are...you telling me that he is..."

Andy continuously nodded his head up and down.

"How do you know?"

"He told the hospital he was your father. And I recognized his name as a champion roper. Then I asked him if both counts were true and he said yes."

It was quiet in the cabin for a long few minutes.

Beau lowered his head and stared wide eyed at the floor directly in front of him. His chest felt like it might explode. When he spoke, it was barely above a whisper. "What's his name?"

"Webber Vance."

Web drove from Jackson Airport to High Point.

An upbeat determination was driving him to be strong and well for this meeting he was about to have with his son. He knew there was a good possibility that he was about to get slammed back down to earth—but if and until that happened, he was going to be positive. He'd been given a gift, he knew, to make this trip in such good spirits. He'd handle the result like a real dad to a young man he'd never had a clue existed. He would leave him with as good a memory as he could make happen. He only had this one chance. *Get it right, Web. Get it right.*

Carly was proud of the way he rallied in strength, after they got off the plane. He'd slept most of the air trip.

She had no idea how Beau would react when he saw her. She tried to prepare herself for rejection. But, regardless, she would give Web and Beau all the time and space this trip could find. They were the most important.

If Beau had nothing for her, she'd live over it. Web, on the other hand—

Her heart rate kicked up until she thought it might jump into her throat as they drove through the High Point Dude Ranch gate. She was breathing hard and realized Web had noticed when he kept darting his eyes over at her.

"Take a deep breath, honey. Everything will work out the way it's supposed to."

She nodded, looking straight ahead. If only she could feel so confidant.

Peggy Patrick

When they stopped at the Brandon's ranch house, Martha was standing in the patio archway behind the house, shading her eyes at their vehicle. Of all people to face first. She stepped out of the rental and gave her a short wave.

"Well, you're a sight for sore eyes, young lady." She walked out and hugged Carly, pounding her on the back with her palm.

Just then, Web stepped out and came around the front of the car.

"Mr. Webber Vance. Good to see you again." She reached out and shook his hand. "I just made fresh coffee. Webber, sit at the table where the umbrella's out and I'll get the coffee." She pointed toward the enclosed patio. "Family's all scattered out today. It's just me here."

Web disappeared inside the half-walled patio. The red umbrella shading the tile topped table was in the far corner surrounded by pots of tall cactus stalks and large tin cans of wild flowers. The atmosphere was just what he needed at this moment. And this lively little woman who he remembered was called Granny Martha was a true breath of fresh air.

Martha pointed across the ranch grounds. "Carly Jones, you need to head on down there. You got business to take care of in the barn. I've seen enough moping around out of that one cowboy to last me the rest of my days."

When she hesitated, Martha gently pushed her that direction. "Go on now. Get it over with." She winked at her then, and turned toward the back door of the house.

"Be right with you, Mr. Vance."

Carly stared at the barn, eyes so wide they hurt. This caught her completely off guard.

The door slammed behind Granny Martha as she came out carrying two smoking mugs. She caught Carly's eye and motioned with a mug toward the barn—"Go on", she mouthed at her.

Why did she get the feeling that Martha already knew she was on the way here? And Webber didn't hesitate to walk off to sit down and leave her standing there. He was never that inconsiderate.

Okay. She was a big girl. Like Granny Martha said, *get it over with.* She headed to the barn with a brisk stride, shoulders back and a racing heart.

Her blonde ponytail swayed back and forth in the breeze. At least she had dressed right—western boots and jeans. Well-fitting jeans. As quick as she thought it, she knew this wasn't at all about what she was wearing.

The inside of the building was dim, but a light was on inside a little room on the other end of the barn. She stood still while her eyes adjusted to the darker space.

A horse let out a squeal making her jump. A couple more whinnied loudly in answer and brought Beau to the tack room doorway. She watched him freeze.

A long silence ensued as they kept their eyes fixed on each other. Then he so slowly started walking toward her, stopping about six feet from her. She watched his eyes travel from her eyes to her hair, then to her boots and back.

"Carly." His voice was raspy and low.

"Hello, Beau."

He had a single leather rein in one hand with an oily cloth in the other. He draped both over a stall rail, then rubbed his hands up and down on his jeans.

"So what are you doing here?"

She said the first thing that popped into her head. "I had to find out—Did they find the cow and baby calf?"

He smiled at that. "Yeah. Andy said she showed up in the front pasture with her baby beside her about thirty minutes after we drove away."

"She nodded up and down. "I'm glad about that."

"Anything else?"

"I came to see you. You look well."

"I *am* well. How about yourself?"

She opened her mouth to say, *just fine,* but closed it without a sound. She came here to find out how he feels about her. And she wasn't a bit fine. Her heart was crushed by the last encounter she'd had with him. He had physically pushed her away from the side of his bed and cursed. The pain that had caused inside of her was as fresh as the moment it happened. But her love for him was undaunted. Even though he had looked her in the eyes when he did it—it was so out of place and character. It didn't fit him and she couldn't make it fit.

"I'm hurting, Beau. I need you to tell me why you did...what you did to me."

He frowned heavily, unable to understand what she meant. "I don't know what you mean. When did I ever do anything to hurt you, Carly?" He took one step closer to her. "Tell me, please."

His expression clearly said he didn't remember. "I came to tell you goodbye at the hospital. You pushed me backward and…" her eyes filled, "cursed at me. I *had* to go, but you didn't let me tell you I intended to come back." Her tears spilled over and she brushed the streams off both cheeks.

He looked as if she'd slapped him. "Carly, I don't remember any of that. I swear to you. I thought you up and left for home without a word to me—as if nothing ever happened between us."

"What *did* happen between us, Beau?"

He stared thoughtfully at her for long seconds as he shifted his weight from one foot to the other. "Well, as I recall, I was given the job of picking you up from the airport one night and I did and *nothing* happened. In fact, you didn't thrill me one bit. Then I delivered you to your wigwam and got a kick out of how appalled you were at having to sleep in it. To be totally honest, I *did* think you were real cute—but, it was that moment when you rushed through my cabin door in the middle of the night—I believe you were being eaten by wolves—and you piled me into a heap of mush in the middle of my own floor."

His eyes began to twinkle with laughter watching her fight to not laugh.

"But—I never…" she began.

"*And then,* you go get me lost in a blizzard and I get sick and you keep a fire going in a cave and feed and water me…" He slowly closed the space between them, "and you wrapped stinky, smelly old blankets around me to keep me warm—and you curled yourself around those nasty covers to keep me even warmer."

He cupped her face in his hands and tilted her head back until her lips were only inches from his. "And—somewhere in all that—*this* happened. He kissed her gently at first, then wrapped one arm around her back, cradling her head in the crook of his shoulder and kissed her until she couldn't deny the *what* that happened.

Finally, he raised his head and whispered, "I fell in love with you, Carly Jones. That's what happened."

"I love you, too, Beau Doss."

"I believe you. But we live in two different worlds. This that you see here is my life. As much as I'd like to tie you up and haul you to my cabin and never let you out of my sight—I can't. You'd have to choose my way of life to be with me, Carly."

"Then, teach me your way of life. Our adventure in the snow storm didn't scare me off. As long as I'm with you, Beau, we can weather whatever life brings us. Haven't I proven that already?"

He searched as deep as he could see into her heart, past the pleading, past the pain, and saw the raw and undiluted truth. She truly loved him.

"Marry me."

Her eyes lit up like holiday lights. "I will. I do."

He laughed with pure joy. "And, I will and I do, too."

They hugged and kissed and held onto each other, rocking and twirling in circles with childish abandon.

"And suddenly—" Beau's face was beaming.

"And suddenly *what?*

"This is what Pastor Judd Luke was talking about last Sunday at Cowboy Church—When God does something special in someone's life, it usually comes *suddenly.* The Bible is full of *and suddenlies.* "

"God is more present than I ever realized. I guess I always believed He was there, but he's been so personal with us." She swallowed and looked down for a moment. "Beau, I had a prayer answered in a big way just—well, part of it today."

"I know, baby."

"No, you don't know about the part I'm talking about."

"Come here." He led her to a bench that set against the wall in front of the tack room. "Now, I want to hear about this answered prayer."

It took her a minute to decide how to bring it up.

"Do you remember a man who was at the hospital—in your room most of the time, named Webber Vance?"

Slowly he shook his head. He didn't remember, but had been told about it. He was quiet. He wanted to know what Carly knew.

"Beau, Webber Vance is—*was* my boss. He was a private investigator in Sacramento."

She watched his eyes widen on her. After a deep breath, she explained how she had been sent here to find out if he was Riley Doss, son of Leonard Doss.

"So—how did you conclude I was him?"

"In the dugout, when you were delirious, I called you Beau and you corrected me. Said you were Riley. For a while, you didn't remember who I was."

She was torn about how much was her place to say, but a compelling to continue seemed to fill her with the words. She gently told him the story that Web had told her sitting in the waiting room at the hospital.

Beau remained silent.

"You were conceived in love, Beau, at least on your father's part. He truly loved your mother."

"What was the prayer that you had answered today?"

"He's...here. He came back with me to see you." She couldn't go any further—couldn't tell him Web was dying.

"Where is he?"

"Martha Walton has him cornered on the patio with coffee.

"Then you go up there and tell him he can go back home. Some things are better left alone. I want *you* to stay. If you do, I'll make arrangements for a temporary cabin for you."

"But Beau—he came to..."

He stood up. "Are you staying?" She nodded her head. "Of course, I'm staying."

"I'll be back late. You're welcome to hang out in my cabin until I get back in this evening."

She stood silent and watched him bridle a saddled horse in one of the stalls, mount up and ride out.

Carly let out a breath she didn't realize she was holding, then fought hard not to cry. *This can't happen this way.* Maybe she should have told Beau his father was dying—soon.

She jumped up from the bench and went into the little room filled with horse equipment. Without any thought, she dropped to her knees and bent low to the floor. *God? Are you here?* Tears began to drip onto the concrete. *Please do something. I will give You my life if You will give Web and Beau theirs.*

She didn't know how to pray the right way and figured she probably just destroyed her chance to get God's help. She didn't know how to talk *thee and thou.*

She dried her eyes and slowly walked back to the patio. Martha and Webber looked at her tear stained face and disappointment came on both of theirs.

Web stood and stepped to her. His arm went around her and pulled her against his side. "I'm sorry, honey."

"Web…he asked me to stay—To marry him. I'm staying."

His eyes grew, along with Martha's.

"Then, why this sad face?" Martha chirped. "And where is he?"

"He rode off. He said he'd be back late." She glanced quickly up at Web and caught the hurtful knowing in his eyes.

"He didn't want to see me?"

She shook her head and stared at the ground.

"It's alright, Carly. I half expected this. I don't blame him. He's had a lot to swallow and some things just don't go down very easy." He covered both of her shoulders with his big hands and turned her to face him. "*This*— you and him—is an answer to my prayer. He's getting an awesome young woman for a wife and you're getting a great guy. After all, he's *my* kid." His grin was Beau's easy grin.

Carly wrapped her arms tight around him and wept into his shirt front.

"Hey now." He ran his fingers through her shoulder length ponytail. "You know me and you can tell him about me when he wants to know. And Granny Martha here picked my whole past life clean. She can tell him—and Andy. Between all of you, he will know me."

Martha sniffled into her napkin and for once, stayed quiet. Life happens, she well knew, and sometimes it's just not to our liking.

"How about you show me where you'll be staying and we'll say our good-byes. I'll catch a flight tonight."

They walked across the ranch yard toward Beau's cabin. Web took in all the sights as they went—the petting zoo, the Indian Village, the party pavilion. He fought off the rush of nostalgia for this way of life—It was painful. He focused on the fact that his own boy had found this cowboy way. He knew he would be happy and fulfilled in it. That was enough.

"This is Beau's cabin. I'll stay in a different one. Or, I'll rent something in town. But, I'll be fine. I belong with Beau, Web. I'll take good care of him."

"I'll be fine, too, sweet girl. I'll leave you here and just be gone." He kissed her on top of her head, gave a final hug and walked back toward his car.

Beau had ridden fast and hard across the back pasture trying to justify his anger. He didn't know who to be angry at. He just was.

His mother wasn't to blame. She didn't want to be a mother. She was young and had two boyfriends to choose from. She picked Doss. Timing. Just crappy timing. At least, Juliette had a father that she knew.

But was it Vance's fault that he wasn't in Beau's life. Neither knew the other even existed. He came looking for him when he heard he was lost. Of course, Carly was lost, too. Maybe he came for her. But, he didn't have to stay at the hospital—or pay his bill. He was here now. He was here—but for how long? Webber Vance was dying. His broad shoulders shook as tears fell.

Granny Martha had gotten Beau an emergency phone number off of Carly's reservation form when she first came to the ranch. It was her parent's number. He'd called, hoping to reach her as soon as he got out of the hospital. Mrs. Jones had told him Carly was staying at the hospital with a Mr. Vance while he had a series of treatments. She said he was in the last stages of cancer.

He let his horse walk back toward the barn to cool out. That's when he saw him.

Web was walking from the cabin back toward his vehicle. He was tall. Thin. Gray hair. Boots. Jeans. From the back, he reminded Beau of himself.

He rode around the back side of the barn and waited in a shaded spot where he couldn't be seen easily. Just as Webber walked past him, Beau reached for his calf rope and made a loop. He whirled it overhead twice and dropped it perfectly over the man's head, letting it fall to his hips before pulling slightly to close the loop.

Web stopped, his shock at the incident lasting only seconds. He turned around and watched his son ride out of the shadows toward him.

Beau stepped down, opened his loop and lifted it over Web's head.

The two men stood eye to eye for several seconds before Beau offered his hand. "I'm Beau."

"Hello, Beau." He shook hands. "Web Vance." If he could choose one single memory to carry into the next life with him, Web knew this moment would be the one. "That's a nice loop you threw. Must have been doing a lot of roping to be so accurate."

Beau shifted his weight nervously, glanced at the rope in his hand, then back up to the man's eyes. "No, sir. Comes naturally. It's in my blood."

Carly stood beneath a tall, cool pine and watched the father and son meet for the first time. With eyes brimming in pure joy, she looked up into the heavens. "Thank You!"

****

EPILOGUE

Everyone was waiting—He just kept staring into her eyes. He held her hands in his, giving this moment all the honor and time that she deserved. Still, it didn't seem real or enough.

Finally, he answered loud and clear. "Yes sir, I ab-so-lute-ly do."

Moments later amid giggles from the crowd, Pastor Luke grinned ear to ear as he tapped the groom on the shoulder and whispered, "Later, Beau. Later."

Beau reluctantly raised his head. "Well, you *said* I could now kiss my bride."

The whole wedding party and guests broke into applause, hoots and laughter.

Best man, Andy, waved his new straw Stetson toward Beau to cool him off before grabbing him and Carly in a tight hug.

It was September in Wyoming. The High Point ranch was closed for two weeks to dude guests to give the families and ranch hands a break. The summer had been long and busy for both High Point and the Double OO.

Until three days ago, Carly lived in a rented apartment in Jackson Hole. She bunked with a delighted Anna Leigh Brandon until the wedding today.

She'd been hired to help Hank with chuck wagon duties all summer—leaving her wondering how he and one little gray granny could ever manage the work load alone. The hours were long, but she couldn't imagine being anywhere else on earth.

The casual wedding ceremony and covered dish reception was the honored couple's request. Just a lot of togetherness and less work was their idea and eagerly accepted by the ranch women who still managed to spread enough food and wedding cake to feed half of Wyoming.

The entire Jones clan was there, along with the Lukes, Les and Kaitlyn Cane and most of their ranch hands and the entire family and extra hands at High Point.

Juliette Doss was there for Beau—her eyes bright with a light that Beau thought he recognized. He felt it in the extra tight hug she wrapped around him just before the ceremony. He realized at that moment that he had never had a hug from his sister. He wanted to ask, but wasn't sure how.

She answered the question she saw in his eyes. "Riley, I could hardly wait to tell you that...I understand now. I prayed to Jesus at a church I attended and I, well, I..."

He hugged her again. "You got saved, Julie."

She nodded, smiling.

"Best wedding present you could have given me. Thank you for telling me."

The noon wedding turned into a full afternoon of celebration, toasts, laughter—even a few tears. As the afternoon wound down and most of the guests were preparing to leave, Jesse clanged an old-fashioned dinner bell that hung from the back of the chuck wagon and motioned for everyone to gather round.

"Folks, this has been a beautiful and blessed day to honor Mr. and Mrs. Beau Vance into our circle of family and friends and their new life together."

Beau went to stand beside his wife and both wrapped an arm around the other.

"But, just one more short announcement—Most of you have walked up the hill to see the new church being built. It should be finished by Christmas and all of you are welcome to come here anytime." He reached for Laura's arm and pulled her close to him. "For those that don't know—our son, Andy, has gifted several acres of his own land to build the beautiful cowboy church building, complete with a riding arena for special events. Judd Luke has pastored out of his home for many years now, and has agreed to continue on in the new church."

"Now, I know that wasn't news to a lot of you here, but Laura and I just learned this morning that Andy has been studying on-line for some time and will receive his degree and be ordained as co-pastor for Real Life Cowboy Church right here at home. *I'll* put it this way—He's had a lifetime of first hand training from this true woman of God right here beside me."

Laura slowly looked up at her husband, realizing what he was saying behind those words. She met his wink and nod of his head with a smile. That was enough for her.

"But, as Andy put it to me—poor old gray-haired Judd might need a break now and again."

The closely bonded group of families and neighbors laughed and hugged. Jesse prayed, most said their good-byes and headed out.

Moments after the last vehicle's tail lights disappeared, Jesse and Laura, Andy, Donny and Reeny and Hank and Martha gathered around Beau and Carly for one last congratulations.

Jesse cleared his throat—hesitated a few seconds. "Beau...Carly, we've saved one last surprise for the two of you. We have to take a short walk up toward the new church."

The couple looked at each other and smiled, excitement darting between them. Holding hands, they followed the group about an eighth of a mile where a new gravel drive had been spread through a thicket of pines, leading to a new double sized log cabin.

Neither Beau nor Carly had seen the structure since it was finished and were impressed with the shiny finish of the logs that glowed under inset lights beneath the extended porch roof. Carly exclaimed over the huge log porch swing, her eyes aglow at the red and turquoise and yellow throws, pillows and silk flowers decorating the cozy scene. She couldn't help hoping their surprise was a wedding night in this gorgeous place.

The group stopped a few feet from the porch and Andy stepped to Beau and held out a set of keys. "This is as far as we go. Inside you'll learn what this is about. But just so you'll know," he looked at Carly, "all your personal things are already moved in there. Enjoy guys—God Bless."

As soon as they were gone, both broke out at a fast pace, Carly squealing, to the cabin—until Beau grabbed her arm and stopped. "Hold the phone there, cowgirl. He handed her the keys, then hauled her up into his arms and practically leaped up the three steps to the front door. After a fit of giggles and three tries, she unlocked the door and pushed it open.

Beau stepped across the threshold and stood transfixed, unable to move for several long seconds.

Both were silent as he let her feet down to the floor in slow motion.

Lamps lighted the combination den and kitchen—an open arrangement where the whole area could be seen from the doorway. The kitchen bar with overhead inset lights filtered a warm yellow glow throughout from wall to wall across exquisite white leather lounge furniture and a mixture of white and natural pine tables and cabinets. The furnishings were light, cozy and warm—complete with braided Indian design area rugs.

But, that wasn't their focus.

Across the den on the far wall, hung a huge painting of Web riding his beloved Rascal. Carly recognized it as the same one that had hung on his office wall, when she had no clue it was him in the picture—a print of it hung on her parent's wall.

Beneath the painting was a wrought iron saddle stand, holding an old, but well kept, roping saddle. An equally old and stiff lariat hung from the saddle horn and looped nearly to the floor over a pair of beat up, worn out boots with spurs still attached to the heels. Beau knew these things had been worn and used by his legendary dad—Webber James Vance.

Carly stood back and allowed him his privacy.

Beau walked up close and lightly, almost reverently, smoothed his hand across the saddle horn. His gaze lifted to the face of his dad—the one who taught him the strength of human love—a lifetimes worth of it in the space of only three months.

During those short months, Web rode alongside his son, roped a few head of calves for the first time in many years, and lived in cowboy style truer than he'd ever done. The chuck wagon food, cattle roundup on the Double OO and sitting around a campfire at night made up his good days. He rested in his own rented High Point cabin, other days.

It was July 10th when father and son spent their last moments together. Beau recalled how the stars that night seemed to be exceptionally silver against the inky sky—the split pine logs popping and crackling in the campfire out beside Beau's cabin.

"I'm not long for this world now, son. But we're both going to be just fine," he'd said.

Beau remembered the light that glittered in his dad's eyes that night as he stared into the firelight—and then said, "I had the darndest dream a couple nights ago. Old Rascal trotted right up to my cabin door over there. I heard him whinny like he always did just before we entered the roping pen. I walked outside and hopped on him bareback and off we rode." Web had laughed then. "I was almost mad when I woke up and found out it was just a dream." Then he'd laughed again."

The next morning, Beau found him in the chair beside the cold ashes of the campfire. He had caught his ride to Heaven in the wee hours of the morning. Beau chose to believe the Rascal he loved so much came for him.

Web was buried, at Jesse and Donny Brandon's insistence, close to baby Bonnie Brandon in their family cemetery on the ranch.

Carly picked up an envelope off of the kitchen counter that had *Beau and Carly* hand scribbled on the front of it. She held it out to Beau. Glancing, he saw both names. "Go ahead, open it and read it."

The letter was Web's shaky handwriting:

May 25th

My dear son and daughter, you are reading this, so I know you were married today. Sorry I missed the wedding, but me and Rascal had some calves to rope. They couldn't wait. These things I left in this new cabin you're standing in are just to remember me by and show my grand babies who their grandpa was.

I ordered this modular log cabin built as a wedding gift. As you can see, it's extra fancy and roomy, so enjoy it. If and when your job for High Point ends, the house can be easily moved. The fancy, by the way, is for my Carly.

Also, the Dually truck I bought, well, that's paid for and belongs to both of you, as well. All paperwork is in the glovebox.

It's tough trying to cram twenty-four years of life into a few weeks, but we did a good job of it, didn't we!

I'll meet up with you two down the road a ways.

Love Dad

She was hesitant to look up at the man she loved and adored more than anybody on earth—afraid she would find the pain of grief, bitter-sweet, maybe—just, not tonight.

But, she found him smiling—all the way into his ocean-deep center. She lay the paper down and met his joy with all the love she could convey in a tight embrace. He held her close and rocked her side to side.

"Know what, Beau? I believe the greatest honor we could pay to Web is to love God and each other with all our hearts and souls. Do you think he would know about it?"

He grinned, then kissed her with all the passion he'd been holding back for months. When she trembled, he reached down and lifted her into his arms.

"I think it's possible. And I also think we should get busy right away with the *loving each other* part. Don't you think so?"

She giggled softly. "I ab-so-lute-ly do."

www.ingramcontent.com/pod-product-compliance
Lightning Source LLC
Chambersburg PA
CBHW022012170626
46808CB00001B/374